# Am I My Mothers Keeper

*YES I AM*

Aileen Read

authorHOUSE®

*AuthorHouse™*
*1663 Liberty Drive*
*Bloomington, IN 47403*
*www.authorhouse.com*
*Phone: 1 (800) 839-8640*



*Published by AuthorHouse 01/15/2016*

*ISBN: 978-1-5049-7319-9 (sc)*
*ISBN: 978-1-5049-7318-2 (e)*

*Print information available on the last page.*



*This book is printed on acid-free paper.*

To my mom and dad
*W*ithout you, there would be no me.
I love you.

# Mom's Dysfunctional Family

My name is Cynthia, and I have a story to tell you about my family. This story is for the people in my life who keep telling me to write a book because sometimes—actually, most of the time—they cannot believe the stories that I tell them. They say to me that if they did not see these things happening to me, they would not believe them, for they are sad, crazy, and unimaginable things. Sometimes I wonder if things like this have happened to other people. When I find myself talking about these things to other people, some will say, "Oh, that's happened to me." But sometimes I shock people with the endings of the stories and their mouths drop open.

When I was about nine years old, I felt that I understood too much to be that age. I believed that I was actually very old. By that age, I went through more than a lot of people, even those older than I was. When I was fifteen years old, Mommy thought I was old enough to handle everything she said to me. She would talk to me about everything, and I think that was my mother's way of escaping; she had no sisters or brothers, and her mother had no sisters or brothers. Mommy said to me one day, "I don't have anyone to help me but you. So please do not fail me." I never thought much about what she was saying; I was just so happy that she squeezed my cheeks, kissed me, and said she loved me. When I think of these moments, I start to cry. Even as I try to write this story now, I can't keep from crying. That day when Mommy told me she needed me, I never imagined that she needed me so much. I was Mommy's second child out of ten children.

Mommy's mother and grandmother were very close to each other. Mommy and her mother lived on Clifton Place, and her grandmother lived across the street. Mommy's mother had only her, and she never wanted any other children, so she kept Mommy close to her. I think Mommy wanted to get away to be with other people besides her mother, but her mother never let her go past the porch when she was a little girl. My mother told me that my grandmother always looked out the window and never let my mother go to anyone's house to play. One time when she tried to walk away from the building that she lived in, my grandmother did not let her out of the house for a month. My mother told me that my grandmother never came outside to be with other people. My grandmother never went shopping; she made my step-grandfather do the shopping. My mother said my grandmother asked her one day what she wanted for Christmas. My mother, then about nine or ten years old, told her mother that she wanted my grandmother to go take her to the park. My grandmother told her no, that she would not take her to the park, adding that there was no good reason for her to go outside. My mother said that every time she asked her mother to come outside, her mother would slap her face and keep her inside for long weeks. Sometimes my step-grandfather would ask my grandmother to come out to buy shoes or dresses for her, but she wouldn't even go with him for that. My mother, at nine or ten years old, would be the one picking out her mother's shoes and dresses—to go nowhere. My grandmother eventually stopped sleeping in the same room as my grandfather. Not once did I ever see my grandfather and grandmother kiss or hug each other.

One day my grandfather went to the store while my brothers Tom and John and I were visiting them. My grandmother asked him to go buy KFC for us to have for dinner, and my grandfather left the house at about four or five o'clock. He returned to the house at about nine or ten o'clock—drunk. My grandmother met him in the doorway screaming at him, and she would not let him in the house. She stood at the door and pushed him out, and then she cut his face with a very sharp knife. I could see the blood going everywhere. I tried to get close to see if he was dead, for she cut his nose from the top and he stopped breathing and fell backward down the first flight of stairs.

She turned around and looked at us, and we ran in the apartment; I started to hide under the bed, but Tom told John and me to hide behind the curtains. The three of us were crying so loudly that she was able to find us and pull the curtains back. She saw us crying, told us to stop, and said to come out from behind the curtains, adding that that she was not going to hurt us. She said she only did this because he was out drinking and that now she had to cook something quick for us because it was late. I heard someone knocking. My grandmother looked out of the peephole. She went to the sink to start washing the knife. I asked my grandmother if my grandfather was going to die, and she looked at me with a sweet face and said no. She told me that someone was out there in the hallway to take him to the hospital, telling us to stay quiet.

My brothers sat down at the kitchen table, and I started dinner with my grandmother as if nothing had ever happened. After dinner, my brothers were sleeping, and I heard the door again. It was now a couple of hours later, and my grandmother still did not answer the door. I watched my grandmother, now feeling very afraid. I thought that if I closed my eyes, she was going to do something to us. But I eventually fell asleep and woke up in the morning, wondering where my grandfather was now. I heard the door again, but this time it was my grandfather with his nose bandaged; he couldn't say much, but he asked my grandmother if he could come in. She said okay. His face looked so pale, as if he'd lost a lot of blood, and my grandmother fixed him some soup; he went straight to bed as if nothing ever happened.

When my mother came to get us the next day, she clearly knew something had happened as soon as she saw us. She went straight to my grandfather's room and asked him what had happened. My grandfather tried to explain, but he just kept telling my mother that it was his fault because he did not bring dinner home and was out drinking. My grandmother told my mother to mind her own business, and suddenly she was reaching up to for mother's neck and choking her. We started crying. My grandmother would always beat up my mother if she said something my grandmother didn't like. She would slap my mother in the face and tell her to leave without taking us with her. Much of the time, we would miss school because of my mother getting beaten up by my grandmother or my stepfather.

Mommy had Tom, John, and Pam, Duke, and me with my father. And she had five more kids with my stepfather: Jack and Jake (twins), Susan, Kate, and Patty. Again, there were ten of us in all. It was always my mother and grandmother in my life, with Tom, John, Pam, and Duke. My grandmother hated my father because my mother was always having children with him but never living with or marrying him. My mother was always leaving us with her mother or her grandmother so she could work. Through most of my first ten years of life, my mother had it hard. She was always moving from house to house because she would get evicted. My grandmother would fight with my mother and tell her to take my father to child support court, but my mother would tell my grandmother that she couldn't find him. Still, for a number of years, she had a baby every year she was with him.

My mother told me she never took my father to child support court because he gave her money. But it wasn't enough to take care of five children, even though Mommy was working as a nurse's aide and cleaning people's houses. My father had a good relationship with me, and my mother would send me off with him when he came around. My father had three children from his first marriage. Then he had Tom, John, Pam, and me, and he left my mother to have my brother Mike with my stepmother. He then left my stepmother and came back to my mother, and they had another baby named Duke. Then he left my mother again and went back to my stepmother. She and I had a good relationship. And all this happened beginning when I was five years old. When my father was leaving my stepmother and my mother, going back and forth with his different women, I would always tell my stepmother when he would come back to my mother. I loved my stepmother and mother, and they were both very much in love with my father. I was ten years old when my father stopped having anything to do with my mother. I didn't see my father as much because I began babysitting for two women named Jane and Anne when I was eleven years old.

We lived down the block from Jane, who knew that Mommy lived in the house with five children and no husband. So I was there for my sisters and brothers when we came home from school. I fixed dinner and prepared all our clothes for the next day because Mommy worked all day, twelve to fourteen hours. When Jane saw that I was taking care of my sisters and brothers while Mommy was at work, she asked me where my mother was all day. I told her she was at work, and Jane told me that she thought I was a very smart and good little girl. When she saw Mommy a few days later, she told her that she thought I was personable as well as great with my brothers and sisters.

Mommy told Sylvia that her grandmother was put in a nursing home because she was eighty years old and getting forgetful. Rather than fight with her mother, she left the kids with me now because we were old enough to help each other. My grandmother and grandfather were getting mad because they didn't see us as much anymore. Tom, John, Pam, and I would take the train from Coney Island to Clifton Place, between Bedford Avenue and Booker Avenue, to visit my grandmother and grandfather. Mommy always had someone watch Duke while we went to see our grandparents. I, with my big mouth, would tell all to my grandmother about how my mother's life had become crazy now.

We left the ghetto of Brooklyn, East New York, to live in Coney Island, which was still nice in 1971. My mother met a women at her job. She wanted my mother to rent with the option to buy. It was a beautiful big house on Twenty-Seventh Street. Mommy was holding down two jobs just to buy this house from the woman. It was the first time I saw Mommy so happy about a house, for she'd never owned anything. She continued working two jobs for a long time, came home, and fell right to sleep. In the morning, she would give me instructions on what to cook and what to wash, and I never saw her until she came home to sleep. Sometimes I would let my friends come over so I could show off our beautiful home to them.

At eleven years old, I never knew that my mother did not own that house. All I knew was that my mother's friend gave it to her.

As time passed, my father came back to my mother again. This time I thought he would stay, for I saw him bring in some boxes and bags. I asked my mother if Daddy was moving in, and she said yes. She was so happy. But one day when I came home from school, I saw my mother coming down the block from the house, crying and unable to answer me. I asked, "Mommy, where are you going?"

She said with a light tone, "I'm going to the store."

When I asked her what store, she said, "Just walk with me." We went a couple of blocks down to the liquor store. While we were walking back home, Mommy started crying again. Things were not looking good to me.

I didn't want my friends to see us like that, so I said, "Mommy, please stop crying outside." I always felt ashamed, because my father kept coming back and then leaving again. That night, Mommy got so drunk that she fell asleep in the tub. I told Tom to help me get her in the bed. Every time Daddy came back and then left, she said she would not take him back again. This time when she said it, I believed her, for I knew this time it was true. That's because I was the one to start Mommy's new but crazy life with my stepfather. The crazy way that my mother left my father was really because of me. I never understood this until I got older.

Now that Daddy was gone again, Mommy began to get her head together. She worked all day again, and I was the boss of the house again. I never knew people were watching my mother's children so much. But Jane was, and she was very good to my mother. She went to bingo every Saturday night. She asked my mother if I could babysit for her three children, Jessica, Ryan, and Thomas, and Mommy said okay. Jane treated me nicely, and her sister and her mother did too. They would come over to our house to spend time with Mommy.

When Mommy told Jane that she was working two jobs to buy the house we lived in, Jane said she would help Mommy in any way she could. Mommy told her she wanted to rent out the basement.

Jane told Mommy, "I have a brother named Rick, and he's looking for an apartment." She said that she was trying to get her brother out of her home because he'd left his wife and was sleeping on her sofa. I'll never forget it because the day that my mother showed him the basement apartment, he never lived in the basement. He moved upstairs in the house with Mommy. Things were going so fast between him and Mommy.

I saw that Mommy was happy again, but something was wrong. She began drinking heavily. Every day after work, she would make drinks for him and his family and friends. Mommy was also arguing with her friend about the house because she was not paying her enough money. She was always coming to the house and telling Mommy that she had to pay her or she was going to take the house back. I was only eleven years old, but I understood; we would be moving again.

One day things got really crazy. Tom got in a fight with a boy who lived in Jane's building, which was down the block. His name was Sam, and his mother was Mrs. Bell. Mrs. Bell came to the house and asked me where my mother was. I told her that Mommy was at work. She said, "When your mother comes home, tell her to come see me."

After I told her I would, she turned back and said to me, "Did you know that your brother Tom beat up my son Sam?" I told her no, and she asked if I went to school that day. I said I did, and she said, "You didn't see any fight between your brother and Sam?" I said no again. "Where's Tom now?" she asked. I told her that I didn't know. She looked at me as if she wanted to kill me. I watched her angrily walk up the block.

When Rick came home later, I told him that Mrs. Bell came and said she wanted to talk to Mommy about Tom beating up Sam. He said, "Don't worry about it. I'll go see her now." He told me that he would be right back, but after about an hour, he still hadn't returned. I looked down the block and saw police cars. I ran out the door, down where the police were, and the police were coming out of Mrs. Bell's house with her and Rick, both in handcuffs.

"What happened?" I asked him.

"When she comes home, tell your mother to get me out of jail," he said.

The police officer who had him in custody asked me who I was. I told the officer that I was his stepdaughter. He put Rick in the car and wrote a telephone number on a piece of paper, telling me to give it to my mother.

When Mommy came home, I explained what happened and she looked as if she'd lost her best friend. She told me to stay there with the kids, and she went to get Rick out of jail. However, she came home without him. She cried all night. I asked her what happened, and she said, "Mrs. Bell pulled a gun on Rick and started arguing with him. She said Rick took the gun from her and hit her on the head. Rick was charged with pistol-whipping Mrs. Bell, and Rick threw the gun out her window. Mrs. Bell was charged with assault with a deadly weapon." Mommy said she had to go back to court the next day to see if the judge would let Rick out.

The judge released Rick, and Mommy later said that she fell in love with Rick more because he stopped Mrs. Bell from shooting her. So she asked the judge to marry her and Rick, and the judge did. Mommy and Rick came home so happy. I remember that Rick's sister Jane and his mother, whom we now call Aunty and Mom, were so happy that they partied all night. Rick had to go back to court sometime after that, but all charges were later dropped.

Mommy sat me down one day and said that she and Rick were having a hard time buying the house. She said that we were going to have to move again. I really didn't understand, but I had a bad feeling because Mommy never wanted to answer the door and the phone. I was very nosy, asking Mommy lots of questions, and she answered my questions honestly. "Mommy, why are you afraid to answer the door and the phone?" I asked her one day. I thought it was because of Mrs. Bell pulling the gun on Rick. I saw my mother talking to my aunt Jane and telling her that she wanted to move away from that block because of what Mrs. Bell had done, but Mommy told me that it was not only Mrs. Bell. She said she could not afford to buy the house, and she said she owed a lot of people money. She told me not to open the doors because people were coming to take the furniture. We didn't have the money to pay for the furniture because she put everything we had on credit. At this time, Mommy was pregnant with the twins. She had to stop working two jobs, and the one job didn't bring in enough money. Now we were moving again, this time from a nice house to a so-so building on Surf Avenue. You could walk out of our apartment and straight to the beach. The rent was cheap, but because Mommy had five kids already and was about to have twins, money was getting tight.

Downstairs under our apartment, we had a drugstore, a ricker, and a record shop. Mommy became the drugstore's best customer. Tom and John had been working there for a long time, and they asked the bosses, Jack and Matt, if I could work there. They let me for a little while, but once Mommy had the twins, I had to be a mother to them. Every time people saw me come outside with them, they thought the twins were my children, but I was only thirteen or fourteen years old at the time. So I was looking like a sad child with no childhood because I always had to babysit my sisters and brothers.

Mommy started to become dependent on pills, and all kinds of medicines were in her room. I knew she was taking pills for a long time for different reasons, but she became so addicted that 50 percent of her money went to pills. Sometimes I wondered which was worse, her pill habit or Rick's heroin and his alcohol. I didn't know much about heroin. Rick would nod in and out of sleep while standing up. Just as his body was getting ready to touch the ground, he would get right back up as soon as he thought he was going to fall. I acted as if it were nothing, for

I lived in the ghetto and many of my friends had one or both parents on drugs or alcohol.

My mother didn't care about his drug problem. She was just happy to have someone who loved her so much. He was a drunk and an addict, but I think he did love her very much. Most of us knew he was on drugs, but none of us talked to each other about it. Mommy talked to me about everything, but she never told me that Rick was a heroin addict. She always screamed at him for coming home drunk, but I know she was really screaming at him for spending most of his money on heroin.

One day he came home from work and said he wanted a car. I heard Mommy telling him that he was always drunk so how could he drive. So he went out and bought a bike from someone. I was babysitting for a woman and man who lived on the first floor in our building. I cannot remember their names. I guess I wanted to forget them, for I saw something happen that still gives me nightmares. The father of the children that I was babysitting for had owned the bike that Rick had bought from someone; apparently, that person had stolen it from the children's father. He saw Rick with the bike and asked him who he bought the bike from. Rick was nasty to him and said it was none of his business. The father of the kids was standing in the alleyway behind the building, and Rick was holding on to the bike. I had been coming down the stairs to go out the front door of the building but had stopped because I heard Rick arguing with this man in the back of the building. When I went back there, I heard the man say to Rick, "Give me back my bike."

Rick said, "Hell no. Give me the money back if you want the bike."

I saw the man go behind Rick, looking around to see if anyone was watching, but he never saw me in the doorway. He was now between the alley and the street with Rick. He then pulled an ice pick out his pocket and stabbed Rick in his side. The blood began pouring out the side of him very fast. Rick dropped to the ground, and I ran to Twenty-Eighth Street and Thirtieth Street, off the boardwalk. I began to scream, and a man knocked on someone's window and said to call the police. I looked down the block and saw the man that stabbed Rick walking as if nothing happened. He headed across the street and into a building. There were a great deal of people coming in and out of the building. When he went to open the door, I was behind him. I put my foot on the door while he was trying to open it, and he tried to punch me. While we were pushing back and forth, I screamed, "This man stabbed my father! Someone please call the police!" Some people tried to restrain him. Before I could turn around, police were everywhere. I think the people that I left with Rick saw me running and chasing the man and told the police where I was running. This crazy man could have hurt me too. But I think because I knew him and babysat for his children, the thought that he would hurt me never came to my mind, and I knew he could not hide, because he lived near me. Moreover, his wife needed me.

Rick recovered fully, and because we had more sisters and brothers, Mommy wanted to move again. This time it was not far. We moved around the corner, in the same building.

When I was fourteen or fifteen years old, I began to notice boys. All my friends had boyfriends, but I could not. Mommy was not letting me outside much, and I always had to take care of the children. I mainly just stayed home. But one day I saw a sailor in a white sailor suit.

Some of my friends later asked what it was that I liked about navy boys. I told one of my friends that I wanted to join the navy, but I loved the thought of having someone who loved it too be interested in me, and his name was JR. I loved the idea of someone telling me that he loved me, and I was looking to get the hell away from my mother, her heroin husband, and all the children she had me take care of. I loved my mother, but I wanted out of her home. I was tired and I wanted to live. Mommy knew JR's sister Missy. She and Mommy hung out at the record shop downstairs on the weekends. Mommy never went far at the time. Still, I was taking care of the kids—Pam, Duke, Jack, Jake, and Susan—most of the time.

When I met JR, he lived on the second floor and I lived on the third floor. My mother knew a girl who had two children and lived on the fourth floor. My mother let me babysit for her two children. She was very nice, but she was hanging out with many people that JR didn't like.

JR and I started dating, and Mommy let it happen. I was surprised that she was okay with that because he was her friend Missy's brother. Or perhaps that's why it was okay. He had just come home from the navy. He was twenty-two years old, and I was fifteen years old. But he started becoming mean to me. He got mad at me one day and told me he didn't want me to be in the apartment of the girl that I was babysitting for. So I told her that JR didn't want me in her home, and she asked him why, but he would not tell her. He only told me that she had many men over. So I stopped babysitting for her because he didn't like it. Sometimes I would get mad at him because he was getting controlling, but I thought he cared for me, so I didn't mind too much.

My mother told me that JR asked her if could he marry me, but she told him not yet. She told him that if I loved him, I would marry him, but he needed to wait a while.

When I came home one day, my brother Tom said that JR was at the door asking where I was. I went downstairs to ask him what was wrong. He asked me if I was in the girl's place, and I told him no, saying that I was standing outside in front of the building. He said he didn't see me, and then he slapped my face. I began to cry, and he told me he was sorry. I was thinking that that he was crazy. I ran home. He came to the door and yelled at me as he knocked hard. I told him to stop yelling; I didn't want my mother to hear him. I told him that I would come downstairs. I was so angry.

# My Own Dysfunctional Family

Because I kept seeing my stepfather hitting my mother, I didn't want to go through this at age fifteen. I couldn't run to my father. I think that at this time, I was wondering why I was taking this from JR. I stayed home most of the day, and that night when my girlfriend was over, I told her that he hit me. She asked me what I was going to do. I begged her not to tell my mother. She led me into the bathroom and took a double-edged razor blade from the medicine cabinet. She wrapped one side with tape, leaving the other side unwrapped. She told me to go downstairs and talk to him. She said she would go down there with me because she was dating his brother Davidi. She went downstairs before me. I came down about a half hour later. JR opened the door and started to kiss me, but I coldly turned away from him. I walked into the kitchen, and he asked me what was wrong. I told him that I didn't like the way he talked to me and that hitting me had to stop because I would not be with him if it continued. "Hit me again," I said to him, "and I'll kill you."

He said, "Who the hell do you think you are?" He slapped my face again. I reached in my pocket and cut him with the razor, but he kept hitting me. Then he looked down at his pants and saw the blood. He turned the kitchen light on and yelled, "You bitch, you cut me!"

I ran to the back room because I knew his brother Davidi was in there with my friend. She had the sheet wrapped around her, and she began crying and screaming. She said to Davidi, "Hold your brother." Davidi asked me what happened, and I told him that JR hit me. He held JR's leg and looked up at JR. Both his leg and arm were bleeding a great deal. I was trying to open the window in order to jump out of the second floor. JR pulled away from Davidi and tried to choke me. I was having a hard time breathing. Davidi saw JR choking me until I was turning blue, and somehow Davidi got JR's hand off my neck. I ran and jumped out the window, landing on the ledge of the building, and then jumped off the ledge to the ground. I thought JR was coming out the window after me, so I ran back in the building and back to our mother's apartment. I had to pass JR's apartment to do so.

Mommy opened the door and saw all the blood on my clothes. I had to tell her that I was okay, that I was not bleeding. She told me to stay still, but I was going crazy because my neck was hurting so much. I went into the bathroom and tried to take my clothes off because I'd been running up the stairs so fast that I'd hit my elbows and knees. I'd also cut my arms when jumping. My mother thought someone cut me. I had to hold Mommy and tell her that I cut JR but I was okay.

While I was in the bathroom, I heard someone knocking on the front door. Mommy answered the door, and it was the police. They took me down to the police station and asked me what happened. I explained to them that JR hit me and I didn't want to be with him like this. The officers turned to Mommy and said, "Why are you letting your child be with this man?"

Mommy said, "There was nothing I could do because she was going to be with him even if I said no." She was right.

The officers let me go home in Mommy's care, but they told Rick that he would be responsible for me because they said Mommy was too easy with me.

JR was arrested for assault and was let out the next day. The judge dropped all charges against him but sent me to an anger management program. Later we got back together, but it was a bad time because he began to use cocaine and marijuana. I thought everything would be okay, but one day he wanted to have sex with me. He was a twenty-two-year-old man, and I knew nothing about sex at the age of fifteen. He forced himself on me, continuing to tell me that it was going to be hard the first time but it would be easy after. So I just lay there and let him have sex with me. I bled so much. I wanted to tell my mother, but I kept it from her. Then I felt that I had to have sex with this man every day just to make him happy. At least I could be away from home and all those kids.

Mommy didn't bother me too much because I was with him, and she looked happy because she knew where I was—right downstairs. She even asked me if I wanted birth control pills. I told her no. The next thing I knew, I was pregnant with Nicole. We would mainly call her Nicky or Bunnie. I tried to hide my belly from Mommy, but she eventually called me asked me if I was pregnant. I started to cry, and I told her maybe. She said, "Okay, I'll take you to the doctor." When the doctor told us that I was between six and seven months pregnant, my mother fell to the floor so fast that the doctor had to give her smelling salts to wake her up. She was crying, but she took me home and we had a meeting with JR. When she told him about the baby, he was surprised too, because although he and I had talked about the baby, we didn't know how far gone I was.

We were moving again, this time across the street to Searise. Mommy had gotten sick of the building by the boardwalk because we had a terrible incident there. The landlord set the building on fire to get rid of the building. People were running out of the building in the middle of the night. Every now and then, there would be a suspicious fire out of nowhere. One day Mommy's fuse box exploded and she reported it to the landlord, but he didn't do anything about it. The fuse box caught on fire again later, and the whole apartment caught on fire. All of us had to move to a hotel. We then moved from the hotel to the Searise Apartments. They were duplex apartments in a nice building. Mommy had gotten lucky to get in that building.

Then Mommy got sick and began receiving SSI because she could not walk. She had osteoporosis and was confined to a wheelchair, but that didn't stop her from having babies. She had Kate and Adriann after I had Bunnie.

I was moving out, into another apartment, down the block from Mommy. Things were starting to look a little bit better in life, but then lots started to happen at once. I dropped out of school to get a full-time job in PathJohn SuperJohnet. My mother's legs were getting weak, so she didn't go anywhere much. When my great-grandmother Mary died, my grandmother became even crazier. My mother had ten children by then, and my grandmother and my mother weren't close. Sometimes they didn't talk to each other for a long time. My grandmother then got sick and died. She didn't even know I had a baby. My step-grandfather came to live with my mother. It was hard to care for my step-grandfather; he was old and losing his mind. One day he fell asleep with a cigarette and burned that apartment. Lucky for us, no one was hurt. Mommy moved out of that building and moved next door, to a building attached to the one she had the fire in. She moved back into that apartment after they repaired it, but there was another fire. While cleaning behind the stove, one of the twins pulled the gas line and the oven exploded. Mommy moved into another apartment in the same building, but I knew the people wanted her out. I was still living around the corner, up the block, and every time I went outside, I heard someone talking about my mother and all her kids in three fires. Thank God no one died in those fires, but I knew something crazy was going to happen with a fire one day.

Life was getting harder for my mother, as Rick was using drugs heavily. I got pregnant again, this time with Georgia. I left PathJohn in Coney Island and started working at Burger King in Manhattan. Being pregnant, it was hard for me to go to Manhattan every day.

JR, Bunnie, and I moved to a bigger but cheaper apartment so Bunnie could have her own room. It was on Bayview Avenue, not far from my step-grandmother. She helped me a lot, including helping me care for Bunnie because sometimes Mommy was too sick.

When Georgia was born, I became a stay-at-home mom. Two months after Georgia was born, she became very sick. The doctor told me she would need a liver soon. When they told me that, I thought someone had shot me and left me there to bleed to death. I asked God, "Why? Why my baby? What did I do wrong?"

She was so beautiful and innocent. My mother told me that God wanted her back so not to ask questions and just accept it. It was very hard to accept something like that.

She died on April 13, 1981, just after her first birthday on March 29. She would never be forgotten. After she died, I started driving myself crazy with drinking and smoking weed. My life had changed so many times, but this was one of the most horrible changes. I thought that there was no reason for me to live. But then I turned to Bunnie and said, "I will go on living because of this three-year-old little girl named Bunnie." Before I had my two girls, I had nothing. Once I had them, I was so proud to have these little babies who needed me, and God knows that I tried my best with them. JR was proud too, but he became mixed up in drugs. Nothing else mattered to him. I had to leave him because things were getting bad between us. He never came home with any money, and he lost his jobs. He was never right in the head after he left the navy. I thought that maybe he had become depressed. He always wanted to get high on all kinds of drugs. When Georgia died, I knew I was finished with him. One day after leaving the house, he came back home high and was arguing with me. I just closed my eyes and threw boiling hot water on him. I pushed him out the door with his skin melting off his leg. I didn't care if I was going to jail. I was just so fed up. Someone heard him in the hallway and helped him to the hospital. I flashed back to when my grandmother cut my grandfather's nose. Was I my mother's keeper, or what? Too many things in my life were happening to me the same way they did to my mother. Like my mother, I moved so many times, and I saw tragedy just as she did.

After JR left, I called my father. He asked his friend to move me into a nice big house. I told my father that I would apply myself and get along without a man. I don't think my father believed me, but he seemed to want to. He moved Nicky and me to Long Island, right next door to him, into a house for rent with the option to buy. I said to my father, "It's only Nicky and me, and we'll make it." I got a good job at TSS, not far from the house.

Bunnie was going to be with my stepmother, so it wasn't too much of a struggle.

JR started looking for me. I never knew how he found me, but I had an idea that my mother told him because she didn't like the idea that I was living out on the island next to my father. One day JR came to my house, and I was so afraid because I had taken his daughter and run away, while our other daughter was in Calverton National Cemetery. She had been dead for only about six months. JR asked me to come back to Coney Island. I told him no. I told him I hated him, but I was confused because my daughter had died. I only had Bunnie, and my daughter needed me. He was on drugs and had nothing. He'd lost a good job and didn't care about Bunnie and me. I let him stay at my house that night, and I slept with him. The next day, I told him to get out of my house. I'd just had sex with my husband, with whom I'd had two children, but he was failing my children and me. At that moment, I knew it was over. He left and went back to Coney Island.

My brother John came to live with me. While John was staying with me, I was going back and forth to Coney Island to see my mother because I was worried about her being sick with all those children. I was going back to my renting office in Coney Island because my mother asked me to. My father didn't know I was trying to go back to Coney Island. One day when John went to work, Bunnie and I were home alone. It was raining hard. Bunnie was in her room playing with her toys, and I was napping in my room. I woke up feeling sick to my stomach. I looked up at the ceiling and said, "God, please do not let me be pregnant." But I knew that I was. I'd been feeling sick since JR had left. I asked God to take this baby from me. Then I went back to sleep, trying to forget the sensation I was feeling in my stomach. The next thing I knew, the ceiling was coming down on me, right on my stomach. I changed my mind and asked God to forgive me. I didn't want anything to happen if I was pregnant.

My father took me to the hospital. I didn't tell him that I thought I was pregnant. The doctor took the urine test and confirmed that I was pregnant. I was very blessed because that ceiling came down hard on my stomach. I knew my father was finished with me. I asked the doctors if I could go home, but they wanted to keep me overnight to be sure the baby was okay. While I was in the hospital, I was thinking, *What am I going to do now?* I went home the next day and told my father that I was leaving the house. He was furious. I told him that I was going back to Coney Island to get back with JR, but I never did. Nicky and I stayed in a hotel for a few months. I called JR, and the two of us stayed in the hotel together, but I was planning to leave him for sure. When housing called me back, Bunnie and I moved in with JR on Second Street.

# Am I My Mother's Keeper?

JR moved in with Nicky and me for a few months, and he was using crack cocaine. I was on welfare, and he wasn't working either. I threw him out of my place. I never saw him again. He knew I was pregnant with JR Jr., but he never helped me at all. Because I didn't want to see anyone, I told people that I was staying at an apartment with a friend. But it was just Nicky and me. I hadn't even told my mother that I was back in Coney Island yet, and I was only three blocks from her. I could go outside and never run into my sisters and brothers because they never came down that block where I lived.

When it was time for me to have my first baby boy, I went to the hospital. Someone told JR that I had a baby boy, but I didn't give a damn. I threw JR from the hospital room, telling him not to come to me and not to ask about the baby. I began to head home alone with JR Jr. in my arms. Then I remembered that I had to cash a welfare check that my friend Laura, who was taking care of Bunnie, had brought to me at the hospital. I had to cash the check to pay the driver of the taxi for the ride home. The cabbie asked me if I wanted him to hold my baby because it was raining outside. I told him, "No, thank you."

When I got home, I was missing my mother, even though she was only three blocks from me. I knew from people that she was okay. People were telling me that John was back with my mother. I heard that my stepfather was using drugs in a bad way now. Things were starting to get more crazy in Mommy's life.

I mostly kept to myself. I had two friends in the building, Grace and Laura, and I had one friend outside of the building, Eva. One day I was walking outside to the superJohnet and I met this guy. Every time I went to the superJohnet, the same PathJohn that I worked at years back, I would see this guy named Marley. To me, he was strange. I didn't understand him. But I was becoming very sad and depressed because I was by myself. I hadn't been with a man since getting pregnant with JR, and now JR was a one-year-old little boy. So I'd gone almost two years without being intimate with a man. I didn't know anyone outside of JR. He was my first love and became my husband, and I just didn't understand the dating life. I was very slow to understand what I wanted. I'd had Bunnie at sixteen, Georgia at eighteen, and JR at twenty—all three children from one man. But even if I stayed married to him, it didn't matter. He had become an addict, just like my mother's husband. I felt I was walking in my mother's shoes.

I decided that I wanted to be with Marley because he was employed and there were good things about him, like wanting his own business. He had plans and goals. I hadn't yet had him over, and he hadn't met my children. I started out by visiting his house, which was very strange. I told him that my mother gave birth to me in the house right next door to him, and he started to laugh. I asked him why was he laughing, and he said, "Maybe this means you were meant to be with me." I had to laugh too because all that time, I was saying to myself that this was unbelievable, but that's the way my life is.

We went to a party, and before I could even get my coat off, I felt very uncomfortable because people were looking at me as if I were strange. I'll never forget it because this was new to me. Marley was from Saint Kitts, and some of the people were from Jamaica. I knew I was the only American in that house. I had never talked to West Indians, and I didn't even understand what most of them were saying. I kept saying, "Excuse me. Please repeat what you said." Marley would laugh at me, but they were nice to me. I started to feel comfortable.

When the party was over, Marley asked me to stay the night with him. I said yes because I truly thought we knew each other enough now for me to be with him. One day he told me that he was going to give a party at his house. He didn't tell me who was coming; he just told me to dress nicely. We met every weekend for four months, and then he wanted to come to my house. I told him no because I didn't trust people and didn't want them talking about me. I didn't want anyone at my house except Bunnie and JR Jr. I think Marley was getting tired of me because I wasn't doing anything with him but having sex. When I went to his house, he started to invite people to be there with us.

One day this guy walked in, and that day my life changed. I was afraid of my feelings about this guy. His name was Kemp, and I said, "What a name." I was in love at first sight. I'd never believed in love at first sight, but something this man said to me made me want to walk out of Marley's life.

Once when Marley and I were making love, Kemp knocked on the door. I ran into the master bathroom. I heard him talking to Marley in the kitchen, and Marley was telling him that I was there. Kemp told him that he was leaving, and Marley told Kemp not to. So Kemp stayed. After I'd dressed, I came out the room. Kemp had this smile as if he'd done something sneaky, and I think it was because he knew that Marley and I were getting down.

Marley gave me instructions to take the train to Eastern Parkway and Utica Avenue. I asked him where his car was, and he said he didn't drive in New York. I thought that was strange because he was a mechanic. But he told me that he fixed cars all day and took the train home. The day of the party, I never thought about the fact that I would be going right next door to the house my mother lived in when I was born. When I got off the train, I was in shock because I had been two years old when my mother moved from that block. I wanted to call my mother, but I still wasn't talking to her. As I said, she never knew I was in Coney Island, right up the block from her. When I started to walk across the street to Marley's, I looked down the block and all around me. I thought that the area still looked the same, but there were more people.

Kemp was sneaky from the time I met him, but I was falling in love with him. I kept telling Marley to stop telling Kemp to come over when I was there, but he didn't listen, and one night Marley did some dumb shit. I was planning to leave Marley's house to go back home on the train, but Marley had gotten drunk and he asked Kemp to take me home. I told Kemp no, but Kemp kept saying that it was okay because he lived near me. Marley didn't know that Kemp had plans to take me from his ass. Kemp told me that he lived in Brighton Beach at this time. I knew something was strange because he said he was living there alone, but I found out later that he was a liar. I learned that the reason I never saw my mother up the block was because she wasn't living there yet. I had talked to Kemp at Marley's house and told him that my mother had many children. The way I talked to him about my mother, he said that I was describing a woman that lived next door to him. But this could not be another coincidence. My life was full of coincidence. Sometimes I asked myself if this could be happening. I was thinking my mother lived down the block from me because someone told me that she was moving into the building on Thirty-Second Street and Mermaid Avenue, but she hadn't gotten there yet. She was living right next door to Kemp. He knew Mommy because of all those kids, and he said I looked just like her. I told him not to say anything to Mommy; I wanted to surprise her. Later I would have the biggest coincidence of my life. Again, was I my mother's keeper? Everything I did turned out to be like my mother or about my mother.

Back to Kemp: Marley got him to take me home. After that day, I never saw Marley again.

## Love at First Sight

Kemp and I were in the car, parked up the block from Marley's house, not far from the Brooklyn Museum. I started to cry in the car with Kemp, and he asked me why I was crying. I told him that I hated Marley. When he asked me why, I told him it was because I knew Marley had another woman. She lived down the block. He asked me how I knew that. I told him that every time I came to see Marley, he would have sex with me and leave me sleeping in his bed for a long time while he was down the block. I think the girl knew about me because one day I came out the house to see where he was going, and he was sitting on a stoop, about ten houses from his, talking to the girl. Every time we got together, he would do this to me. One day the girl looked down the block and told Marley that I was standing outside. So he came to me and asked me if I was okay. I said yes, but I asked him why he was always running down the block and leaving me in the bed. He never answered me. He just said to go back in the house, adding that I looked tired. He was right. I was always tired.

In my mind, I did not belong with Marley. He was so strange, and I couldn't figure it out. But that night Kemp took me home, I'll never forget what happened. He reached over and touched my hands, saying, "Marley is not for you." I asked him why he was saying that. He said, "Because he's going back to Tennessee."

"What's in Tennessee for Marley?" I asked.

"Another woman," Kemp said.

I said, "That's it. Let's go home, Kemp."

That night I had him drive me to my friend Eva's. I told Kemp to wait for me. When I came downstairs with my children—Bunnie was five and JR was one by then—Kemp asked me if they were my children. I told him that they were.

JR jumped right into the car like a big boy and said to Kemp, "What's your name?"

Kemp was so surprised that this child could talk so well at one year old. Bunnie never said a word to him. I told him to take me to my home now. He could probably see in my eyes that I wanted to cry again. When we got to the building, I asked him to come upstairs. He told me no and asked me where my husband was. I told him not to worry about him because I had filed for divorce and it had been over between he and I since JR was born. I'd never taken any man to my house, mainly because of my children, but Kemp was someone special. I knew this. It was late at night when I walked into the building with him, which made me happy because I didn't want anyone to see him yet.

I spent time every day getting to know him, and one day I said that I wanted to go see my mother. He said okay, but we always had something to do.

It was Thanksgiving 1983 when I met Kemp, and I never looked back. It was now early 1985, and I was pregnant with Kemp's child. I hadn't wanted to get married to Kemp yet. I wanted to watch him and see what he was about because I was very much in love with him. I eventually started getting suspicious of him with other women.

# Brothers and Sisters Back

I was now about eight months pregnant with Sunny, and I wanted to see my mother. Thank God I went one day with Kemp. For the first time in a little over two years, I got to see her. She would soon be moving into an apartment right down the block from me. For the time being, she was living in a basement apartment with Duke, Jake, Susan, Kate, Patty, and Rick. Rick looked terrible, like a heroin addict. Mommy wasn't walking very well; she was in and out of the wheelchair. In the basement apartment were only two rooms: the kitchen and living room. There were no bedrooms, and the bathroom was in the hallway. All seven of them were sleeping in the small living room.

I started to cry and asked Mommy where John, Pam, and Tom were. She said that the three of them were living somewhere else, with other people. Later I found out Pam was living in a shelter because she and the girl's father separated. Tom was all over the place, and I didn't find out where he was living. John was back and forth too. I never knew John would eventually be closest to me. I think that when Mommy got sick, he was closest to her.

I was so happy that I soon had my mother, brothers, and sisters next to me. I knew they were happy too because now they had space, including four bedrooms.

I was about to give birth to Sunny. I told Kemp that I would give Sunny time to walk and talk, and I would then be going back to work. I had had babies every two years. I was now twenty-four years old and about to have my fourth child. While giving birth to Sunny, I asked the doctor to tie my tubes because I did not want any more children, and the doctor did just what I wanted.

So I was soon home with four children and hadn't worked since my two girls were born. I was tired of living in the projects and always being broke. I'd had enough of staying home. I thought that if I put my mind to work, I could get out of this depressing life. I told Mommy that I wanted her to take care of Sunny. She agreed, and Mom and Rick's mother helped me.

When Sunny was a year old, I got married to Kemp. I was a lot happier with myself because I got my divorce from JR. I was also happy with Kemp and the kids as well as being next to my mother. I hadn't seen my father yet, but I was planning that visit too. I wanted to work, and I asked Kemp to get me a job with a taxi company called PDQ Car Service. I don't know why I wanted to drive a taxi, but I figured I had to do something to make good money for my kids.

## Too Much Coincidence

Something unreal happened. The radio announcer said that a tragic accident had occurred. A woman in a wheelchair tried to save her husband from a heart attack, but she could not lift his body from the bed to the floor to lay him flat and give him mouth to mouth. He died, and the ambulance couldn't reach him because it crashed on the way to him. He never had a chance to be saved. And no one ever questioned those two guys who were in the room with him. One of the guys died, and the other was never seen again. But I think the police didn't care; they just labeled them.

Rick was a poor black man who died of a drug overdose in the projects in the ghetto. I don't think they even did an investigation into his death. At this time, I felt sorry for Jake because he really went through hell finding his father dead like that. I think Susan was hit hard because she was proud to have her father home, even though he was on drugs. Even though he had a drug problem, Mommy truly lost her best friend. She never got over the strange death of her husband.

# Death and Life

Life changed again. John came back home to Mommy; Pam came back from the shelter because she had to help Mommy with the girls. Georgia had died, and Rick had died. What next? This was an important time to get my life together. The DOT hired me to work as a traffic agent writing tickets—or, as I called it, a brownie. I didn't understand how this job could cause so many problems. People would spit at you, hit you, and even stab or shoot you. They parked illegally, and they wanted to hurt you. Sometimes I would come home drunk just to forget this job. I thought driving the taxi was a problem, but being a brownie was scary.

Kemp and I started to have problems because I bought a new car, a red Ford Thunderbird, and my friends wanted me to go out with them because I had the car. I was the stupid one because I let people tell me what to do with my car. Some of my friends didn't give a damn about me. Some just used me, and some just hung out with me because I worked with many people and therefore knew where all the action was. I was a mess while working for traffic; I wanted to get out of this job, but I had to look for something that made more money. I had a dream that I was going to buy a house and let my mother stay there. I thought about it every day, but one day my dreams began turning into nightmares.

I was on the list for bus operator, and I told Mommy that I was going to buy a house and get her out of that apartment, but something terrible happened. Rick had been dead now for about four years, and I was getting ready to spend this Mother's Day with Mommy. In the morning, Duke came to my house. He was usually with me, as was Jake, but Jack was in a group home. For some reason, he and Mommy could not get along. Duke and Jake had been in the same group home, but Mommy let Jake come back home because she said he was now listening to her and doing well in school. But she said that Jack and Duke never wanted to listen to her after Rick died. I didn't know what was on their minds.

Duke, Jack, Susan, and I were sitting in the living room, and Nicky, JR, Sunny, were talking about what we were giving Mommy for Mother's Day. Jack had come down from upstate, and he was going to surprise Mommy. Susan had just come down the block from Mommy's house and was asking them to call me because my mother's house was on fire.

I couldn't believe my ears, and I didn't feel my legs. I dropped to the floor. Duke started to run out the door, as did Jack and Susan ran, but I told Bunnie to stay with her brothers. When I got downstairs, Duke drove, and we got there fast. We all looked up at Mommy's room, as it was the only room burning. We were screaming because we knew that if she was in that bed, then she had no chance. We had to run up six flights of stairs. One by one, we all reached the top. At Mommy's door, the neighbors told us they were sorry and news crews were flashing lights in our faces. Someone screamed, "Here are her other children!" I grabbed Kate, and Susan grabbed Patty, but it was so fast that I didn't understand how the news got there so quickly. "My God," I kept saying. "My God, please tell me my mother got out." One of the neighbors shook his head. A firefighter held me, and then Kemp and Amy held me because I could not feel my legs. I asked how the fire started. Susan said that she didn't know, that no one knew. Kate was so scared that she didn't immediately tell told us what happened.

Later that day, Kate said that Mommy asked her for some coffee. She said she turned the coffeepot on and asked Mommy if she wanted her to make her coffee for her. Mommy told her no. She said that when she came back in the room, the coffeepot was on fire. She said she could not put the fire out, and she tried to grab Mommy, and Mommy told her that she was tired, to leave her and go get help. She tried to lift Mommy, and the fire was getting bigger. Mommy was too heavy for her; she couldn't get her out of the bed. Patty went to the door because someone was knocking. Patty said that when she opened the door, the person asked her what was going on, but Patty became afraid of the person because she didn't know him, so she closed the door. And she later told me she looked out the peephole and thought the person knocking was Kemp, but when she saw it was not Kemp, she closed the door. But that was not the end. Kate tried to put the fire out herself. I felt so bad for these girls because they were my baby sisters and they went through living hell. At this time, I was the one left to take care of them. I never knew what to do with all of them.

I just took it one hour at a time. Not even one day at a time; that was planning too far ahead. I had to plan my mother's funeral and take care of Duke, Jack, Jake, Susan, Kate, Patty, Kemp, Bunnie, JR, and Sunny—not to mention myself, number eleven. I went from having three children to having nine children. And if Georgia were alive, I would have ten children to care for. Was I my mother's keeper? I *was* my mother's keeper. Now my biggest problem was how to keep all these children. I had a two-bedroom apartment. I had my sisters and brothers on my living room floor. I never knew if my brothers and sisters appreciated me. I took them from Coney Island to get them away from the building where Mommy and Rick died. Two tragedies happened in their apartment.

I got a transfer out of my building and moved to the Bronx. I lived there for nine months and did not like it. I called my father and asked him to help me because I had to get out of the three-bedroom place that they gave me.

# Change and Chances

I got my father to talk to his friends about renting me a house with six bedrooms, two kitchens, three bathrooms, and a huge yard. The kids were happy for the first time in their lives. I look back at the pictures that I took of them. They had bikes and other toys that they never had before because my mother and stepfather could not afford these things for them. What a cruel life these poor children had.

Right now they were happy, but there were a lot of problems with the children emotionally, which was normal for the kinds of things they had to go through. Things would soon change again.

Later the boys moved out, and I had to give the girls to Pam. She lived in Harlem. Susan, Kate, and Patty didn't like living with me because they didn't like my father. I never knew why they didn't like him, but they wanted to live in the city. They said they didn't like living on Long Island, and they loved Pam. And I had to leave the big house because the landlord was losing the house. I was paying her nineteen hundred dollars a month for the children to be happy, and they didn't want to live with me.

Kemp, Bunnie, JR, Sunny, and I moved into my father's trailer. We'd gone from living in an apartment in Coney Island until my mother died to an apartment in the Bronx that was too small for the kids to a big beautiful house to a four-bed trailer. That was the way life went. My father then found my family and me a three-bedroom house at 32 State Avenue in Wyandanch, the Long Island ghetto, but my children were home and happy again. I was still working for DOT, but my husband couldn't find a job, so I was stuck with the bills and the rent.

Bunnie met a boy named Germaine. He was a nice kid, but he and she were fifteen years old. When she got pregnant, I wanted to die. I was feeling like my mother again. I was my mother's keeper.

No one could ever tell me I wasn't. None of these things happened to my sisters. Everything in my life was similar to hers.

The landlord of our house said he wanted to sell the house, but we couldn't buy it because Kemp didn't have a job. He'd been a mechanic since I'd met him, and I took him from Coney Island, where he had a good job. I'd moved him so many times for the kid to be happy, and now I wasn't happy.

I told Bunnie I would help her take care of the baby. My grandbaby's name was Oscar. I loved this baby very much. It was a good feeling to look at him. He made you forget all your problems. Now I definitely had to get a better job. We also had to move again. We were going to Phoenix Road, right next door to my father, but it wasn't such a great move because the house was old and needed so many repairs. However, the area was nice and had good schools.

When Oscar was almost a year old, we learned that we could not stay in the house. I was thinking of moving back to Brooklyn, to an apartment, because I was the only one working. Kemp could not find a job in Long Island. The transit authority was calling me to drive a bus, so I really wanted to get back to the city and save some money. This was a chance to buy my house and stop moving all over like my mother had. We found an apartment on Rutland Road in Brooklyn. I hated Brooklyn, but I would save my money and buy a house for my children.

Once we were in Brooklyn, Bunnie started giving me a lot of trouble. She began seeing a kid named Bob. I didn't know where she was going with her life. I guess I shouldn't talk. She appeared to be making the same mistakes as my mother and me, but I was going to try to stop her from doing so. I knew she was going to leave me because Bob's father had a house. I had plans for Nicky to go to college, but I think that was all going down the toilet. She had her own plans, but they didn't look good. She was moving too fast with Bob. She was staying out all night. Sure enough, Nicky told me that she wanted to leave and live with Bob. He could throw her out on the street anytime he got mad at her, and believe me, he was going to get mad at her because she was a very hard person to deal with. She made all the wrong moves when it came to important things in life. She didn't care about anything. She had her own way, and she listened to no one. Then she got pregnant again. She was living in Bob's basement, which looked like shit. I put her in the Allen School after she got her GED, and that was a waste of my money and time. But I couldn't be thinking about her at the time, only about Oscar and buying my house.

I had saved fifteen thousand dollars, and my husband couldn't believe it. He had God on his side but didn't know it, for I stuck by him while he cheated on me so many times. Now he was seeing a woman who was friends with his mother. I had someone telling me that he was cheating on me, but I couldn't reveal the name. I promised the person that I would never tell Kemp who told me. Kemp crashed our Chevy Lunar while coming from a hotel with this girl. The person that he hit called me and told me that he had an accident in my car with his witch, but I still stuck with him, crazy ass me.

I was ready to close on my house. I was going to rent a truck and move my family to their own house. I went from having nothing but four children and no education to driving a bus for NYCTA and owning my own house. I was so proud of myself. I'd pulled myself out of the ghetto. Now I felt like a person. We would be living in a nice area of Queens, Cambria Heights. I had to change my bus route.

Bunnie didn't come with us to Queens. She was staying with Bob in Brooklyn. I knew this relationship with her and Bob would not last. She was so young, as was Bob.

I saw Oscar every weekend, the only time I had with him. He was now old enough to go to school. Nicky was having problems with Bob, and I was thinking she had no choice but to give Oscar to me. She had a job, but that was not going to last, for she never stayed at a job long.

My problems with Kemp were getting bad. When I met Kemp, he was dating Molly's sister Jadi. Then I found out later he was dating a woman named Selene; that woman was crazy. She lived next door to my mother in Brighton Beach. The woman had a nephew who was Kemp's good friend, and she was after Kemp. Every time I went to my mother's house, she came out of her house to talk about Kemp to me, and I always told her that I didn't want to hear her. Now I found out that Kemp was going out with a girl who lived across the street from me. It was too much of a coincidence. Her child went to school with Bunnie. Thank God these people didn't get to me, for they came before me. But now that he was with me, I saw that Kemp really was a cheating motherfucker. He could not stop cheating on me. The first time I caught him cheating on me, I wanted to beat the hell out of him. He was flirting with my friend, who turned out to be my babysitter. I tried to beat her ass every time I saw her. Then he cheated on me with a girl my brother dated. She was trash and a cocaine head. When we left Coney Island and moved to the Bronx, I didn't find him cheating on me there. Maybe I just didn't catch that one. When we moved from the Bronx to Long Island, I thought he was cheating, but I never caught that one neither. But now that we'd moved to Rutland Road, he came home with these pictures in which he was holding Ms. Fat's niece.

# Home Drama

I know for sure about her. She was the one in the accident with him coming from a hotel. He confessed about that one—but only because I found out about that from a reputable person. Now that he was in Queens with me, I hoped that he was going to be a good person. He left that girl in Brooklyn alone but went around his brother's friends and started sleeping with one of his brother's girls, but I never knew until the day I came home from work and someone called me to tell me that my truck was in the yard down the block from them. I had many friends, and one of them lived down the block from the girl named Sandra. I was thinking about Kemp going to this girl's house. He always said he was there because his brother was friends with these people.

One day I got mad at Kemp because he lent our truck to his brother, which I'd told him not to do this because his brother drove like a madman and always got into accidents. I knew his brother was going to screw up my insurance, and he did, but not with this truck. I went to the girl's house, and I knocked on the door and told the girl's mother that I was there to pick up my truck. The woman knew who I was, but I didn't know who she was. She became very nasty to me. She said, "Who are you?" I told her that I was Kemp's wife and wanted my truck. She said she wasn't giving me the truck, because Kemp wasn't there. So I got on the phone and called Kemp, telling him to tell the women to let me take my truck out of her yard. She told Kemp that she was not giving me the truck until he came there. I told her that I was not waiting for Kemp to come home because I had to go to work later. When I told the woman that I was calling the police, she went in the house and then came back to the door. She began waving a machete at me and telling me to get the hell away from her door. She was smart and never stepped outside. When the police came, they did not arrest her, because I told them she never came out of the house with the knife. They told her to get the keys to the truck, which she in turn told her daughter to do. Her daughter was laughing at me, and I told her that I knew she was screwing my husband. The police asked her what she had to do with my husband. She lied and told the police that she was not with my husband but with his brother.

Later I would learn that my husband got this girl pregnant. She and Kemp had sex in my bed. Sunny told me that the girl was coming to my house at night. When I went to work, my neighbor saw this girl coming out of my house at night. Kemp was a real motherfucker. I told my friend Deana about Kemp cheating on me, but I don't think she cared. I then told my friend Britany and my sisters and brothers. I was so hurt that my husband could not stop sleeping all over the place, with anyone. I was thanking God that I didn't have AIDS. I was furious because he had no reason to cheat on me. But I also knew that he was a sex addict like his father. I was told that his father had children all over Jamaica. If I stayed with Kemp, I would be a jackass.

I met this beautiful man named Egypt and fell hard for him. I was driving the bus, and he boarded one day when I was coming from the store where I shopped for my lunch. The people at that shop were all his family, and he was a deli boy. Everyone in that store hated me because I was married to Kemp, and he told all of them that I was married. I really wanted a divorce, but Egypt started beating me, and I wanted out of his life. One day he thought I was talking to Kemp on my cell phone, and he beat me bad. I contacted my lawyers to get a divorce. The papers were drawn up and just waiting for me to sign, but I had to keep Egypt in this country. So I asked him to stay. This was the craziest time of my life.

Kemp didn't give a damn about me because he was with Sandra and she was pregnant. Still, Kemp kept coming back to the house, and he was a nasty motherfucker. He would have sex with Sandra and still went to have sleep with me. I fought with Kemp every day because even though he moved out, he still had the key to my home. I burned the sheets and some of his clothes on the lawn and almost went to jail for that, but the police felt sorry for me when I told them that I found my husband sleeping in my bed with another woman. I was moving out of the house to stay with

Egypt, and because he kept coming there, Kemp knew I wasn't staying in the house. I told him to stop coming to the house.

We had taken out a home improvement loan because we needed many repairs, and the day I got the check, Kemp and I went to the bank to cash it. While we were out, one of my neighbors called me and told me that he kept seeing Kemp let this girl out of the house at night. I asked Sunny if this was true, and he said yes. Now I was ready to kill Kemp.

When we came back from the bank, I told Kemp that I was leaving the house because I found out about him and the girl. Kemp locked me in the house with Sunny and told Sunny to go downstairs. He kept me in the house all day. He was telling me that he was going to kill himself and my son and me. He had a nine millimeter and a shotgun. He would not let me leave.

I waited for him to fall asleep and then ran out of the house. After finding a pay phone, I called the police and told them that he was holding me with two guns. They blocked off our entire street and called the house, but he would not answer. I told them my son was in the house, and the police tried calling his cell phone. He didn't answer. While the police were telling Kemp to come out of the house with the bullhorn, he didn't respond, and I knew it was because he was not in the house.

Sunny soon came to the door, and I screamed to the police not to shoot my baby. I ran to the door, and the police grabbed Sunny and me. I asked Sunny if he was okay, and the police asked him if his father was in the house. He said no. He said his father left the house when I did. Sunny said that he went out the back door and got into his Jeep. I asked the police if they could trace his cell phone, and they did. He was calling from the Springfield area. I told them that I knew he was calling from that bitch Sandra's house.

# Egyptian Nightmare

I went with the police officers to Sandra's house, and there was his Jeep parked right around the corner from this bitch. When they went to the Jeep, the police let the air out of his tires. I started to look around for him because I felt him watching us. Then I looked across the street and screamed to the police that he was right there. He was standing there watching us as if he'd lost his sense. I didn't like what I saw. He looked crazier than he had when he left the house in the morning.

It was late at night when the police locked him up. I had to go to the police station to press charges against him, and I was feeling sick because then I knew my life with Kemp was over. We'd met in 1983 and had a hard life together for fifteen years. After all we had been through, I still loved him. I couldn't just turn off my feelings for him, but after he pulled that gun on me, I also hated him. Many people told me that he had a lot of balls bringing that woman to my bed. Because he knew I moved my clothes out of there, he tried to tell people that I didn't live there, but I owned that house. He was living with Sandra, yet he refused to stay away from me. I was paying all the bills for that house because he was not working.

When he came out of jail after the first time I had him locked up, he stayed away for a long while. He went to live with Sandra, and she ended up getting pregnant. All the while, he was calling me and telling me that he was not going to stay with her. I told him that I had a man now and didn't want anything to do with him. He asked me to stop seeing Egypt. I told him the truth, that I was in love with Egypt and that he was crazy if he thought I was leaving him. That really pissed him off, and one day he surprised me by waiting near the house to see if I brought Egypt there. I pulled up to the house and went in, and he came running in after me. Egypt was preoccupied with something in the car, and he never saw him enter the house after me. Once I saw Kemp, I asked Sunny to call the police because he'd seen Egypt sitting in the car waiting for me. Kemp was screaming, "I'm going to kill you!" Sunny started screaming and begging his father to put down the knife he was holding. While Kemp was holding me down on the floor, Sunny was pulling Kemp off me. Minutes later, Egypt came running into the house with a lug wrench. He pulled Kemp off me and told him that he was going to bash his head in. Kemp pointed the knife at Egypt, but the police came just in time to stop him.

The police put Kemp in the patrol car and said, "Leave your wife alone or you're going to keep going to jail." Kemp looked at Egypt from the police car and told him that he was going to kill him.

I asked Kemp why he kept coming back here. "Just stay away from me. Go back with Sandra and be happy."

He got out of jail because I did not press charges. I felt sorry for his lowlife ass. This made Egypt angry, and we began having problems. When he saw that I refused to press charges against Kemp, he asked that I divorce him. As much as I loved Egypt, I did not feel in my heart that I was ready to divorce Kemp, so I was honest with Egypt and told him that I would not. That was the first of many times that he hit me.

Once Egypt started hitting me, I began planning how to leave him. I thought I was in love with him, but his true colors began to show. I realized that he was very mean. Kemp never hit me, but JR always did, and I knew that I did not want to relive that shit that I had with JR. I told Egypt that I was in love with him, but he knew that I was also still in love with Kemp. I thought Kemp was a very sweet and loving person, but he was also a cheater and a huge liar. He lied about everything, and you never knew when he was telling the truth. The cheating and the lies made me hate Kemp so much that I contemplated killing him on many occasions. When I got with Egypt, I was trying to make Kemp mad and pay him back for cheating on me. Then Kemp went and got Sandra pregnant. The funny thing is that I knew that both Kemp and his brother were sleeping with Sandra. Neither one of them believed that the other was sleeping with her. I knew very well that Kemp was sleeping with her because one day when I came home with JR, Kemp was acting like a big kid and I told him to get the hell out of my life because he kept staying at the house while he was with Sandra. One day he would be with her and then come back the next day. He screamed to me that Sandra was pregnant and that he would be coming home, so I got mad and told him to stay at her damn house. He said that he wanted me to sell the house and give him his half of the money. I told him that I worked for this house and he had not had a job since I brought this house, adding that he wasn't getting shit. That's why he would not leave. I told Kemp that it was very mean and low of him to tell me that Sandra was pregnant in front of JR. I knew from that day that Kemp did not care about me or anyone else. He was trying to get me mad at him, and it was working because this only made me hate him more.

He played me like a young kid and didn't think before he acted. He was a very low-class person. I knew I should be looking away from him, but my stupid ass helped him plan Sandra's abortion. He came to me and asked me where she could get rid of the baby. He cried to me and told me that he did not want to be with her and that he wanted an abortion. I told him that he was going to hell for putting that damn bitch through this. I hated her for screwing in my bed. My son Sunny was home with him and that bitch. He was screwing her in my bed while my son was listening. That is why I hated her and him, the stupid ass. I guess I was a real ass too. Kemp played around with Sandra because I caught him with Ms. Fat's niece, and that's when I fell in love with Egypt. Then he left that one to gets this ass Sandra pregnant.

I was seeing other people. He did not want me to tell that to the counselor. The counselor told Kemp that that's why we were in counseling together. Kemp was ordered by the court to go to counseling, and I thought it would help if I went with him. He was in court because I locked his ass up for pulling those guns on me, but that didn't stop him from still being with Sandra. Now I was trying to leave Egypt. Because we were in counseling didn't mean I would be taking Kemp right back. My job and plans were to keep him calm because he liked guns.

After we'd attended a couple of session with the counselor, she asked me why I was with Egypt and Kemp was with Sandra. Kemp told her that he was trying to make me mad. I told her I was with Egypt because I found out about Miss Fat's niece, and after I got with Egypt, I fell in love with him because he treated me like a woman. So I packed my clothes and moved out of the house and into Egypt's apartment. Kemp stayed in the house. I never changed the locks, and he never changed the locks on me. I then started to hear about him and Sandra, so I knew I was moving on without Kemp. We would come back to the house to get clothes and leave, but every time we ran into each other at the house, Kemp would stay and ask me for sex. I would tell him to go to hell and go back with his baby mama. He would act as if nothing were wrong between us. I told him that we were living separate lives now and he should just move on. He told me to sell the house and then he would go. I told him never. So we kept the house, and he kept coming back. He screamed to me that Sandra was pregnant and that he would be coming back to the house. We argued every time we saw each other. I stopped going to counseling with him because I knew it was a waste of my time.

Sandra got him an apartment, and she moved out of her mother's house and in with him. She was about two or three months pregnant, and he came to me and told me that he wanted to come back home. He asked me where she could get an abortion. I told him about Choices, and he got on the phone and made the appointment for her. He told me to drop him at her house because he didn't have a car at the time. I stood right there when he made the appointment for her, and when I dropped him at her house, he turned around and kissed me and told me that he was getting rid of this baby so that we could be a family again. I told him that he was going to hell because of this baby.

Kemp told me to go home, but I waited down the block to see if he really was going to take her to have that abortion. He came out of the house a half hour after I dropped him off, and someone came to pick her and him up in a little white car. I followed them to Choices, and he went inside with her. I went in and stayed far away. There were many women in there, some for pregnancy tests, some for abortions, and some for checkups. I knew because I asked the guard at the front desk if I could make an appointment to get an abortion, and he told me to go through a door on the left. I didn't want to go through that door because Sandra and Kemp had gone through that door.

While I was in the hallway, I asked the guard what time they closed, and at that moment, someone came out the door. I could see Kemp with Sandra, filling out paperwork. She was asking him questions, but I could not hear them because I was too far away and I did not want them to see me. I then got mad and walked over to them. I said to her, "So now you're going to have an abortion with Kemp's baby? This is my damn husband. You are a nasty bitch, and you are going to hell for this." She told Kemp to get me out of there or she would not go through with the abortion. I screamed, "Are you sure it's Kemp's baby and not his brother's? You were screwing him and his brother." Kemp began pushing me out of that waiting room. As I was heading out the door yelling at Kemp, I used the camera I'd brought to take pictures of him and her. This was proof enough for me to get a divorce from Kemp.

While I was snapping pictures, Kemp had his hand in the air, pointing at me and yelling, "Go home, Cynthia! Stop this!" He said that she would not have the abortion if I stayed. "Please," he said. "Please go home." I turned just in time because I saw Kemp's eyes. He looked so sad, but he was also trying to tell me that the guard was getting ready to grab me. I slipped right out of his hands and ran like hell. I was crying all the way to my car that I'd parked four or five blocks away. I couldn't stop crying. It was about nine or ten in the morning, and I had to be to work at four. I took the film to Rite Aid to be developed and get some Tylenol. He'd fucked my head up so bad, and Egypt was calling me all morning, but I didn't answer. I went to the house to sleep, and Egypt was at the door looking for me at about twelve thirty.

I'd never forget this day in my life. Before I dropped off the film, I'd called Kemp's mother and told her that she never believed me about her son having been with Sandra but that I had pictures to show her and Sandra's mother. Sandra's mother knew she was with Kemp because she put up bail for Kemp when I had him arrested.

The first time Kemp was locked up for pulling a gun on me, a friend of ours put bail up for Kemp. I knew because they told me. The second time I had him locked him up, for pulling a knife on me, Sandra's mother bailed him out of jail. I knew this because Kemp told me. Kemp was living with Sandra and her mother when he didn't have a job, and she got her bail money from Kemp's second case because I dropped the charges on his ass. Kemp was upset that Sandra's mother took his Susu money for him living there. She got tired of him living there, so she asked one of her sisters to get him an apartment. The next thing he needed was a car when he got the apartment because he had to find a job while he was with Sandra. I helped him buy a car from Sandra's friend to get Kemp's ass back to work. I did not do this so that he could help me out with the house but so he could keep his apartment and not need to come back to the house.

The morning after Sandra got rid of the baby, I called Kemp's mother to tell her that I had the pictures of the two of them in the abortion clinic. I called Sandra's mother too and told her that her daughter was in the abortion clinic having an abortion with my husband's baby. She screamed at me over the phone and called me a liar. She told me that her daughter would never get rid of her grandchild. I told her that she was the liar and gave her the address so she could see her daughter there getting rid of her grandchild. I told her that when Sandra got home, she wouldn't feel well so she should watch her. I'd never had an abortion, but I had friends who had, and I knew she might be sick as hell.

I got nasty messages after that on my answering machine because someone was mad at me for telling about the abortion. I went to work after Egypt yelled at me. I had told him that I wasn't feeling well, and he'd told me to stay home with him, but I didn't want to stay with him at home because all I could think of was whether Sandra really did get rid of this baby; I was planning to get rid of Kemp if she didn't. I was upset the whole day. My mind wasn't on driving that day, but I couldn't call Kemp because he didn't have a phone at that time.

When I got off work that evening, I told Egypt that I didn't want to stay with him anymore. He was mad as hell, which I knew he would be. This was why I called him opposed to telling him to his face. He kept calling me at home, but I didn't want to hear from him. I wanted to hear from Kemp. Late that night, Kemp called me from Sandra's house, and he told me that he made sure that she got the abortion. He said that she was very sick and was suffering. I told him that she was not suffering yet. He said that he would see me tomorrow; I started to cry because I was so in love with him and was so happy that she got rid of the baby.

A few days later, Kemp called me and told me that he was getting rid of his apartment and moving back into our house. I told him to be sure of what he was doing because I'd hurt Egypt's heart and was not staying with him anymore. He was happy that I'd come back home, but he began to lie to me again. One day I was off from work, and I hadn't told Kemp my days off. I was watching him. I told him that I wanted to try to make things work between us. I think that when he was telling me that he loved me, he was lying to me again. He went right back to Sandra's when he gave up his apartment and I gave up Egypt. He was leaving the house one day, and I followed him. I couldn't believe his car was right in front of her house. This motherfucker made me look like an ass. I had JR and Sunny in the car with me. I took the club lock apart and yelled for Kemp to come out of the house. He didn't come out, so I broke the front window of his Jeep. That's when the front door to the house opened. Kemp was standing in the doorway telling me to stop or he was going to call the police. I told him to call the fucking police because they couldn't lock me up for breaking my own car windows. I went to the side and broke two more windows, and as I started to break the fourth window, he was standing there eating off a plate as if nothing was happening. All he said was, "Cynthia, why are you doing this to me?" As I was deciding whether to break the fifth window, he went in the house to put the plate of food down.

He came out of the house and jumped in the Jeep while I was trying to break the fifth window. As he drove away, I got back in my car to catch him and bash his head in. I was laughing and crying at the same time. JR and Sunny were in the back of my car asking me to stop. I was yelling at Kemp as another car passed us, and the man driving said, "Lady, what's wrong?" I told him to call the police because that man stole my car. The man began to chase Kemp for me, but we both lost him.

I went right back to Sandra's house because I believed that's where he would go. When I got there, the police had just come up behind me. I was yelling to Sandra that I was going to lock Kemp's ass up again. The police told me to stop yelling and asked Sandra what happened. Sandra told the police that I broke up her boyfriend's car, and an officer turned to me and said, "Is this true? Did you trash her boyfriend's car?"

I said, "Yes, it's true. He's her boyfriend, but he is my husband and that's my fucking car. I want to lock him up for stealing my car."

The police told Sandra that she couldn't call the police on the man's wife for trashing their car. The police told me the car belonged to both my husband and me and that I couldn't lock him up for stealing the car. He told Sandra to go back into her house. She told the officer that she wanted me locked up. He asked what I did to her, and she said nothing. The officer told her that she was a lucky lady because this woman could kick her ass for being with her husband. She told the police that she was not sleeping with my husband, and they called her a liar because she'd referred to him as her boyfriend. The police told her that they would send me home so that I could not hurt her.

The officer came to me and said to get into my car and go home and try to forget this man. He said not to come back to this house because he could arrest me if I did. Then he said that he was very sorry to hear that my husband had done these things to me but to take the children out of this mess. He told me to start planning a divorce. I thanked the officers for not locking me up.

I knew where I stood with Kemp. Now I did not want anything to do with him. The next day he called me, telling me that he loved me and that he wanted to be with me, saying that he would go tell Sandra that. He asked me to drop him off at Sandra's house and watch him. He said that he was going to get clothes that he'd left there and that he would tell her in front of me that he was coming home to me. He apologized for making me mad enough to break the windows. I told him that he was standing in her doorway eating her food, and he interrupted me to tell me that it wasn't her food, that he brought food and was eating it there. I told him that he still didn't come out of her house when I called him. "You acted like a nasty person with no regard for your family. You were standing there when you weren't supposed to be there. You told me you were finished with her. So you have clothes there now? Let's go get those clothes and tell her that you are coming home to me now."

When we got to her house, he got out of the car and told me to wait in the car. I looked up at the window, and I could hear her saying, "Go home. Don't tell me anything. Just go home to your cheating wife." I could hear her yelling with her Jamaican accent, "Kemp, she is with the next man, and if you want to be with her and her next man, go—just go." When he came down with his one bag of clothes, I told him that he should have just left the cheap bag of clothes. I saw her stick her head out and close the curtains. She looked as if she was crying, but it didn't bother me. I wanted to kill that bitch for sleeping in my fucking bed and allowing my son to hear them.

I went home and asked God to forgive me for coming back to Kemp. I asked God to help me with him, and for a while, things were quiet, but I had one problem: Egypt. He would not leave me alone. I had a car service business with him, and my mistake was letting him use my name for the hack license. He got tickets for using the car as a dollar cab business. He called me one day and said that we had to go to court. I told him that I don't want to go to court and that just when I thought shit would be quiet for once, it started all over again. I said to myself that I would be better without children or men because someone's problem was always catching me in the middle. First the car problems with Egypt, then the immigration papers with Egypt. I helped him because I thought we would be together, but that was his fault because he hit me for nothing.

One day I'd asked my friend Tina to help his ass stay, and she spent his money and used him but did nothing to help him. He lost track of her and wanted me to play detective and find her. I found her one year later. After she married him, she went down South to live with her grandfather. I took a chance and went there with Egypt. I didn't expect her to be there. I thought I would just go ask her grandfather where she was, but to my surprise, she answered the door. She asked me what I was doing there fucking with her grandfather. I told her to come out of the house, but her grandfather did instead and told us that the police were on their way for us. I told the old man that we were not there to start any trouble. I told him that her husband was outside and wanted to serve her divorce papers. She said, "Get the fuck away from my door."

Egypt said, "Come outside, bitch, so I can kick your fat ass."

As I began to pull him away from the door, Tina's grandfather shot an old gun at us and the gun broke into pieces. She hysterically asked her grandfather if he was okay. He replied that he was fine, but the gun broke in his hand. Egypt and I ran down the stairs, and Tina came out of the house with a broomstick. I turned to kick her in her ass, and she pushed me down, knocking me to the ground. Egypt then punched her in the face. She was acting like a madwoman. Every time she tried to hit us, we got her down. We let her go when the police came.

The police asked her what was going on, and she said that she wanted us locked up for harassing her grandfather. Egypt gave the police officer the divorce papers and explained that he was trying to give them to her but she came out of the house to fight us. She told them that we hit her. I showed the officers the hole in her screen door and told them how her grandfather tried to shoot us with an old gun that broke into pieces. Then I explained how she came at Egypt with a broomstick. The police officer told Tina that she would go to jail with us until they did an investigation. That shut her up. She told the officer that she did not want her grandfather in jail. She said that she just wanted us away from her door. The police gave her the divorce papers, and we never saw Tina again. One day Kemp saw Tina, and she told him that she had a hit out on me. Kemp said that he told her that if anything happened to his wife, he would come for her ass.

Once that was over, I asked Egypt what he was going to do now that he was divorced from Tina. He said that he was going to wait for me to leave Kemp. I told him to listen to the lawyer, and he said that the lawyer did not know what she was talking about. One day before we found Tina, we'd gone to his lawyer to file for divorce from Tina, and the lawyer asked him why he'd married Tina and not me. The lawyer told Egypt that I knew everything about him. He asked the lawyer how she could know that, and she said that I had the answer to every question she asked him. He told the lawyer that he did not marry me because he could not marry me since I was already married. The lawyer told Egypt that every time I came to the office with him, she could see that he really loved me. He replied, "But Cynthia does not love me." The lawyer then asked me to step out of the office so she could speak to Egypt privately. I knew that when I left the office, the lawyer would question Egypt about our relationship and me. When Egypt came out of the office, I could tell that he had been crying. I asked him what the lawyer said to him, and he told me that the lawyer told him to leave me alone quickly, before I broke his heart. I asked him what he said, and he said that he told her that his heart was already dead from what I did to him. That is why I told him to listen to the lawyer, but he still kept his hopes up high.

On the day that we were driving to court to take care of the tickets from the car service business that we had together, I was upset with him because he knew that I was back with Kemp, but I just never came out and said it to his face. I just stopped having sex with him and stopped going out on dates with him. As we were driving to the court on Atlantic Avenue, we were talking, and he stopped the car out of nowhere at the foot of the Verrazano Bridge. I asked him why he stopped, and he said it was because he wanted to screw me up. I was crying but otherwise kept quiet. I could not speak or do anything. I sat there scared as hell. I didn't know what to do. I jumped to the back of the Mazda minivan, and he followed me and began to beat me in my face. He told me that he beat me because I left him like a bitch. At this point, I thought that my nose was broken; blood was everywhere. As soon as he started to move the car again, tears rolled down his face. He picked up a club and threw it at me in the back of the car. It hit me in the arm because I put my arms up to protect my face. He kept looking at me in the rearview mirror while I cried. I don't know how he knew what I was thinking, but he said to me, "Go ahead and jump your dumb ass out of the car while I'm driving." That was my thought, but I did not want to get hit by the other cars that were behind him. My plan was to wait until we got into the parking lot to escape.

We got off the highway and turned into a parking lot that was wide open and sunny. I could see the parking attendant looking at me as if he wanted to ask me what happened to my face. I looked at him pointedly, trying to give him a hint to call the police, but I guess Egypt's look of "Mind your business" was stronger because after looking at him, he seemed scared to look at me. Egypt held my hand while he paid the parking attendant. He whispered to me that he wanted to get me some ice for my face because he knew he could not take me into the court looking like he just beat me up. When we walked over to the court, he told me to stand in line while he went to get ice. As soon as he turned his back, I ran like hell and never looked back. I ran to my car and told the parking attendant to give me the car. He did not ask me any questions and gave me the car keys.

I drove to a police station a few blocks away from the Manhattan Bridge. I made a police report, and a warrant for his arrest was issued. They asked me if I needed to go to the hospital, and I told them no. I just went home, and the next day Egypt came to my house. He was knocking on the door like a crazy man, and Kemp was in the garage in the backyard. I was talking to my friend Audrey as I opened the door. Egypt grabbed me. He was crying hard and kept saying that he could not be here without me. I said, "Egypt, go home and stop this because the police are coming for you." He told me that he did not care and that he would go to jail for me like Kemp did. He began to walk to the back of the house, and I yelled to my friend that Kemp was in the garage. I tried calling the police, but Egypt went to the back and cut the telephone wire. I ran to the back of the house with Sunny and Audrey and her son, and we saw Kemp come at Egypt with a machete. I yelled for a neighbor to call the police. I was so ashamed because the neighbor asked who Egypt was, so I lied and told her that he was a crazy friend who was fighting with Kemp. Here I was, where I never wanted to be—between my love and my husband fighting—but I knew that it could happen when you played with someone's heart.

Egypt moved away from Kemp, and the neighbor told Egypt that the police were on their way. Sunny was holding his father, the roles turned because he was protecting his father. Egypt started walking up the block crying. I tried talking to him, but he kept walking away from me. I asked him to please forgive me and go on with his life and to forget me. I told him that I hated him for beating me as he did. I told him I could never be with him after that.

When I returned to the house, the police were there talking to Kemp, and I explained to the officers that I left my husband for abusing me, but we were trying to work it out, and while we were not together, I was seeing someone else and my husband was seeing someone else. The person that I was seeing came to talk to me, and I didn't want to talk to him. The police officers looked at each other and laughed. They said that I'd better decide who

I wanted to be with because a lot of people could get hurt. They filed a police report, and after that day, I did not worry about Egypt. I did not fear him anymore because I think he understood that we needed to stay away from each other.

One day while driving my bus near his apartment, I saw him step into the street right in front of my bus. I slammed on the brakes so hard that people flew everywhere. I thought I was going to hit him for sure, but thank God I did not. The people on the bus were yelling out the window for him to get the hell out of the middle of the street, and I maneuvered my bus around him and continued my route.

After that, he continued to call me and ask me how I was doing. I told him that I was doing okay, but he knew I was not happy with Kemp. He knew that Kemp was very sneaky. I never knew if he was going back with Sandra, but I was still talking to Egypt. Kemp knew it. I didn't want to have sex with Kemp; I missed Egypt. One day he asked me to go with him to look at apartments to get out of the house he was staying at with his uncle and family. I found him a nice apartment and slept with Egypt again, causing myself problems. I told Egypt that I was not going to marry him and that I was not going to leave Kemp. Only the sex was good between Egypt and me. Egypt gave me the keys to his new apartment anyway.

Kemp answered the phone one day, and it was Kings County Hospital asking for me because Egypt was in the hospital. He gave me the phone, and I asked them what was wrong with him, but they would not tell me over the phone. They said that he had my number in his pocket. I hung the phone up, looked Kemp in the eyes, and asked him if he did anything to him. He said no, but I didn't believe him. I put on my clothes, and Kemp asked me where I was going. I told him I was going to the hospital. I turned around and told him that I really hoped that he did not do anything to him.

When I got to the hospital, I found Egypt hooked up to so many machines. I asked him what happened, and he said that when he got out of his car, he felt dizzy and fainted. Someone called an ambulance. The police thought that he might have been shot because he was a taxi driver in Brooklyn, but the EMS confirmed that there were no bullet wounds. They did not know what was wrong with him, but the doctors wanted to keep him overnight for observation. He went to sleep, and when he woke up, he asked me to move his car and bring it next to the hospital because it was on the meter and the next morning he would get a ticket. That is when he told me that we would have to go to court again for more tickets that he got on the car.

One day after he got home from the hospital, I was sleeping at his apartment and a Spanish girl called. She left a message on the answering machine: "Papi, where are you? Call me back. I'm worrying about you." I laughed because I thought that she had the wrong number. The phone rang again, and I answered. She asked who I was, and I told her that I was Cynthia, asking who she was. She did not answer me but asked why I was at Egypt's house. I asked her why she was calling Egypt's house, and she told me she was his girlfriend. I told her that was funny because I was his girlfriend too. She said that she knew who I was and that he told her that he did not have anything to do with me anymore. I told her that was funny because I was here in his apartment while he was not answering his phone. She asked me where he was, and I told her that I didn't know. She said that she had been beeping him and calling him but hadn't been able to reach him. Apparently, they were together for a few months. He told her that he had to leave me because I was still married and that my kids were spoiled brats. He said that although I gave my husband and kids everything, they did not give a shit about me. I told her that it was all true, but he and I were still together. She told me that she loved Egypt but she knew that he still loved me. She asked why I didn't stay with him and marry him. I told her that I did not want to marry him or have anything to do with him at this point. I explained that I was out of touch with him until I got the call a few weeks ago that he was in the hospital. I went to see him, and when I returned to the hospital the next day, he was not there. I asked him how he got home, and he said that he drove himself. When I asked how he felt, he said he felt fine. He said that the doctor gave him blood thinners so that his blood could flow easier. I told him that I hoped he felt better and that I would always love him but I needed to live without him. He told me that he loved me too. I didn't know about these stupid ass men anymore.

Months went by and not a word from him. I changed my number. The date that we had to go to court for the ticket was approaching. When I got into the TLC office, many people were there fighting tickets, so at first I did not see him. He came up to me and startled me because I had not seen him in a long time and I was there by myself. I did not like the way that he looked. He had gotten so skinny. He told me that I looked good, and I told him that he didn't because he had lost a lot of weight. He told me that I did too. "Tell the lawyer you're here," he said.

He was talking to some guy and told him that I was his ex-girlfriend. The guy started laughing and asked him what he did to let such a nice girl like me go. Egypt told him that was the problem: I looked nice but was not nice. I told Egypt that he did not have to tell that man that because he did not know me. He told the guy that he was lucky not to know me. I got up and went to sit behind them.

The lawyer came out, and our case was called. When I got in front of the judge, he scolded me and told me that I could not allow Egypt to drive my taxi as a dollar cab. Then he suspended my hack license for ninety days. We left the courtroom to wait for the paperwork in the hallway, and I told Egypt that I had to take the license plates off the car. He asked if he could hold on to them a little bit longer. I told him no because I didn't trust him. If he did something wrong again, I would have to come back to this court and face the judge, who could take away my commercial license. When I told him that he was going to make trouble for me, he pushed me and knocked me on the chairs. I fell between a couple of chairs, and people began to grab him. I tried to get up and fight back, but the guards were trying to hold him. He got away from them. One thing I forgot to mention about Egypt is that he was a very strong man who was well trained in martial arts. He was running out of the door when the police tried to pull on him; he pulled right out of his shirt.

The police took me to my car, and I called Kemp to tell him what happened. I was still so upset, but I told him that I had to go to the house with the police to get the plates off the car. The TLC police gave me a complaint number, so there was no problem getting the plates. I just had to hear Egypt's bullshit.

I went home and showered to wash away the crazy day. I heard someone knocking on the door, and my sister Kate, who was living with me at the time, answered it. She called, "Cynthia, Egypt's at the door!" I put some clothes on quickly and came to the door.

When I asked what he was doing there and said the police were looking for him, he said he didn't care. I told him that Kemp was in the garage, and he said he did not care. Kate got upset and yelled for Egypt to go away. He pleaded with me to talk to him. I told my sister that I would walk him to the corner and talk to him. I told her to call the police if I was not back in ten minutes. He pleaded with me to let him keep the car for a few days longer because he was not doing well, and I knew he was not, so I said, "Okay, one week." He kissed me on my head and thanked me.

I knew I had to do something quickly because he was crazy. I let him have the week that he wanted because I knew he was taking care of that Spanish woman and her three kids. That's why he looked thin. They were making him tired because he was not used to having to take care of so many people. His eyes looked dark, as if he never slept.

I had to do what I had to do because a week passed and he did not bring the plates. I went to the nearest police station to have a police escort to get the plates. After explaining the situation to the captain, he sent a patrol car with me. Egypt came outside and asked for more time. The police said that I did not want to give him more time. That is when he went off and screamed that now that I had my husband back, I did not need him anymore. He said that he helped me when Kemp fucked up my life and now I wanted to fuck up his life. I explained to Egypt that I was not leaving the plates with him, saying that I did not want any more tickets. I told him that he would not let me do this to him. The police were very nice and told him to go get the plates and stop talking to me that way.

Egypt came to the car and apologized in front of Kemp for speaking to me nastily. I told him that I helped him because he caused me to lose my hack license and now he wanted me to lose my CDL. I told him that I did not want to hurt him but to make sure no one would sue me. He looked like he'd lost his best friend, and that was the last look that I ever saw on his face. I missed him very much, but I didn't miss him beating my ass.

I remember the times that Kemp was watching Egypt and me. Kemp came to my bus stop one day to talk to me, and he and Egypt got into a fight. I didn't want to see them kill each other, but I think Bunnie was responsible. Kemp told me that he always was able to find me, thanks to my own daughter. Kemp paid her for information, and she ratted her own mother out. I didn't know about that girl.

She saw the things Kemp was doing to me, but she always helped Kemp go against me. JR didn't like Egypt either, but Sunny really loved him because he was like a real father to him. He was the father image that Kemp was not to Sunny. Egypt did a lot for Sunny in two years, and Kemp never did anything with Sunny.

Things began looking a lot better between Kemp and me. We were together again for a while with no problems. This was good; finally my life was quiet, but as you know, it does not stay that way long. Kemp still did not have a regular job and worked out of our garage in our house as a mechanic. Sometimes he made good money and sometimes nothing at all. I was able to keep up with the bills, but I began having dizzy spells. When I went to the doctor to find out why I was getting dizzy, I was diagnosed with vertigo. I had never even heard of vertigo before, only the movie. But I believed that my life was a movie and that's why I was getting dizzy. I was soon unable to work because I couldn't drive the bus dizzy. I was home going crazy. I was losing my credit cards. Kemp wasn't working much, and I had to struggle with bills. He could come up with the mortgage, but we will still struggled a great deal. Without my work, our life was a huge struggle. God helped us through this, and my vertigo was under control so I could go back to work.

I got a motorcycle, but I could not ride it because although I was feeling better, I was not cured and still experienced dizzy spells. The motorcycle was a gift from Kemp after I left Egypt alone for good. It was the most exciting gift I ever received. It was the best big boy toy ever. I was in love with the motorcycle, although I hadn't cared for them when I was younger. It was when I turned forty that I decided I wanted my own bike. My children and father thought I was crazy, but I was always safe. Thank God I never had a bad accident on the bike.

# Making Good Money

I was afraid of sitting home doing nothing, so I went to the library and studied real estate. I always wanted to sell real estate. My goal was to be like Donald Trump. I was reading everything about the real estate Johnet. Now everything I did was about real estate. I loved to talk about real estate and motorcycles. I guess that because I was so poor, I became my own educator. I only had a tenth grade education, but I was able to say that I could make a lot of money with my self-taught education. I was very proud of myself. I was out of work, but when I got back on my feet, I would survive. I would go for my real estate license. I had been out of work so long that I was ready to go back. The eight months of not working in 2000 was pure hell. Now that I'd bought my house, my goals for when I was doing better was to keep it and retire happy.

It was finally time for me to go back to work, and I was so happy because I needed the money after being out of work for so long. As I promised myself, I went to real estate school. Transit was good because I was making sixty thousand dollars a year, but I wanted to make one hundred thousand or more. I knew that with my goal as a real estate agent, I could and would make it. I took the real estate exam and passed. I was so proud of myself for achieving this. This is why I believe that anyone can do anything that he or she truly wants to do. Now I was a licensed Realtor selling houses to anyone who needed one. I made great money, so naturally I wanted a change.

I loved my house in Cambria Heights, but my pride had me wanting to move on to some other area. The area that I always loved was Long Island because of my father. My goal was to buy a house a little bit bigger and detached. I wanted a backyard for BBQs. I never had a big backyard for all my brothers and sisters. I always loved my brothers and sisters, and I missed them so much. I have to say that my family was just as crazy as any other family, but Mommy was blessed with all of her children. All ten of us were doing very well. My mother did not have a good life when she was alive, but she was surely looking down at her children now and saying that she was proud of us. I know she loved all of us, and I loved my siblings very much. I think Mommy gave us the best gift in the world: each other. I'm especially grateful for John. He was the brother everybody wanted. Now that I was looking for a new house, I would give my current house to my brother John for all that he had done for me.

Before I move on, I want to mention that I was planning to go to Germany and Holland. My cousin Joe was another best buddy in my life. I always wanted to travel, and now that Joe was living there, I could take the trip. I wanted to take Kemp, but that wasn't the best time because he had many problems and wasn't interested in traveling anymore. However, I was not going to wait for Kemp to travel. He'd already gone to Holland and other places. Although I thought he was finished with traveling, I was just beginning.

Once I visited Germany and Holland, I did not want to come home to the United States. I loved it in Holland and needed this vacation very much. I spent a week there, but it wasn't enough time to see much of anything. I did get to see a fair amount, though, thanks to my cousin Joe.

# Life's Ups and Downs

I went to Dusseldorf, Koln, Morheim, and Frankfart, and we ate in five different restaurants, enjoying German, Turkish, Greek, Spanish, and Italian cuisine. Joe also took me to Holland. Something nice was planned to do every day, and I was treated like a queen. My cousin was the best, as was his girlfriend Jane. They treated me so well and had great friends too. I think there was a reason for me to get out of the United States to see places other than New York. It made me want to move from there or at least travel as much as I could. I wanted to go back as soon as possible. My life had changed so much.

I had a lot of trouble with Nicky. She moved in with me in September of 2004 and moved out in February 2005. Living with her was the worst time in my life. She came to me because she was living in an apartment that she got when she left the shelter, and she made a mistake by bringing her friends from the shelter. She did go to college, but she quit. I don't know what was going on in her life, but I do know that she looked bad. She was very thin and unhappy with the way her life was. She didn't like anyone or care for herself enough to get her life together. She never stopped picking men who did nothing for her but give her more problems. She had no job, no house, and no car. While she was book smart, that was a waste because she wasn't even working. She didn't even care for her children. I had Oscar most of his life, and Nicole had poor Armani, but she left her with all the fuck-ups so she could run the streets with the lowlife people she knew. That's why I told her to come live with me.

There were times when I sent Kemp to get Armani and she was with all of Nicky's stupid low-class friends. Sometimes when I went there, Nicky was paying Bob's mother to keep Armani, which was a shame because that was her grandmother. I told Nicky to come stay with Sunny, Kemp, and me. I said that would take care of the kids while she worked. I was working two jobs, driving for transit and selling real estate. Kemp was still working from the house as a mechanic, and Sunny was working at Target. Nicky made a fuss when she had to get up in the morning and take the kids to school eight blocks away from the house. But we picked the kids up after school.

Nicky said that she was looking for a job, but she was going out there looking for that jackass boy in the housing projects. Nicky didn't cook breakfast, lunch, or dinner for those kids. She got up in the morning and screamed at those kids like they were dogs. She would be out all day and come back late at night. She would wake up tired and moody from getting Kemp all day. When she was drunk, she would be very nice and funny. However, when she didn't have money or her think ass honey, she was a witch, especially to me and her children.

One time Nicky didn't come home for a couple of days. She kept calling Sunny to ask him if the kids were okay because she could not get over that bum Billy. He lived in the projects with his mother and had kids all over the place. When she finally came home after two days of drinking on the streets with assholes, I was sitting on the sofa braiding Armani's hair. I asked her where she was and why she wasn't able to take care of her children. She turned and said, "Bitch, I don't have to answer you. I'm grown, and I don't have to say shit to you." I jumped off that sofa and grabbed her. I began beating her ass. She was crazy to talk to me that way, as if I weren't her mother. She talked to me like I was a bitch on the street. She made me feel as if I were shit, and I had flashbacks of my mother getting beat by her mother. I was going to beat some sense into her head.

Sunny came in the house to stop me. I knew it was going to be bad because Sunny cared a lot for his sister, and that day he went against me for her. He picked me up off her and threw me to the other side of the room. Sunny was mad and started yelling at me and asking if I was crazy. I picked up a mug and threw it at him, but it didn't hit him. He picked up the mug and threw it back at me, so now I knew he was mad enough to hit me for her. I went into my room and locked the door because I wanted to call the police; I really thought Nicky and Sunny would gang up on me.

When the police came, I explained the problem to them and told them that I was mad because my daughter was going out and getting drunk and not coming home to take care of her children. The police told her to leave, but she said that she wasn't going anywhere. One officer said to her, "Yes, you are. You're going to one of your friend's houses." She was mad because she didn't have any friends and the people she knew were tired of her because she always argued with everybody. She finally left, and I was stuck with the children again.

The house was quiet for two days, but then Uncle Moe died, and my cousins Joe, Lamar, and David arrived. We planned to cremate Uncle Moe. When David went back home, Joe and Lamar said to come to Philly with them to get away from all the problems at home. Kemp and Sunny said they were going to help me. They would take care of Oscar and Armani. I left and went sightseeing in Philly with Joe and Lamar. It was the first time I had been to Philly, and it was nice in some places.

When I put the key in the front door after my two-day vacation, along with my cousins, I didn't know what I would see. I called for Sunny, but he didn't answer. Then I called out for Oscar; he didn't answer either. I looked in my bedroom, but no one was there. No one was in the kitchen or other bedroom either. I headed down into the basement. That's when I saw the children sitting on the bed, and I knew Bunnie was in the house. I said hello and asked what was going on. Oscar said nothing, and Armani wouldn't look at me. I asked the children where their mother was, and Armani said she was in the bathroom.

When she left the bathroom, I asked, "Why are you here?"

She just looked at me. I said, "Your friends don't want you. And when are you going to clean this nasty house?" She didn't answer me. I asked her what was going on, but she still didn't answer me. I asked if she was drinking in the house with the kids there. She asked if she looked like an ass to me, and she went to lie down on the bed. I told her that since she was there, she could clean the nasty house, adding that she didn't do shit there. I told her I saw a mouse upstairs and that she had my house looking like a pigpen.

She stood up on the bed and said, "You just like fuckin' with me and you can't leave me alone!" I grabbed her by the neck and couldn't stop choking her ass.

My cousins came running down the stairs trying to stop me. "Cynthia, stop please!"

I heard Lamar say, "Cynthia, she isn't breathing." But I didn't care because I was tired of her bullshit. Finally I stopped, and I could see my fingerprints on her neck. The kids were crying, and I told Joe and Lamar that I wanted her out of my house because I couldn't take it anymore. Still, I hated to know that I almost killed my daughter in front of her children. They were so afraid of me, and I was very sorry for them to see this, but I was doing this so she could take care of herself and them. There were so many problems in my life, and Bunnie gave me more that day. She called the police on me. The police came and talked to her, and then they came in the house to talk to me. I said that she was getting drunk in front of her children. They told me that there was no evidence that she was getting drunk in front of the children and that there was evidence that I choked her. They said that I should have gotten a restraining order to keep her out of the house but I didn't. So now I was going to jail for assault with intent to kill.

When I was walking out the door, she was clearly happy, but the kids were crying. I saw my friend Tori coming through the door. She had called me when the police were outside talking to Nicky. I told Tori that I knew they were going to lock me up but I was not afraid.

Tori pleaded with Bunnie not to press charges, and Nicky said that she did not care about me because I kept hitting her like a little child. She told Tori that I didn't like anyone who was poor and that if she didn't drive a bus, I would not like her. She told Tori that she had a hard life with me and that Tori didn't know the things that she went through in life. She said Tori that I put her through hell. I knew that Nicky was a spoiled child because I gave her everything. When I looked back at her childhood pictures, I could see a happy child, and I worked all my life to give my children better things in life. My children were never in a shelter, homeless, or hungry. They had it better than my brothers and sisters and me. We had nothing but each other and our grandparents. Thing were very difficult. Bunnie didn't know what having it hard meant.

When Bunnie had me locked up, I think she wanted me to lose my job, but I was very good at my job and not even Bunnie could make me lose it. When I was leaving in the patrol car, I told her that she'd better be out of my house when I returned. The police officers were nasty to me, and I heard Bunnie telling them that she was not getting drunk, that she was planning to be a police officer. I think they believed her.

I didn't get out of jail for two and a half days because the arresting police officer hid my folder. I think the cops did that to me because I told Nicole in front of them that she'd better be out of my house when I came home. So they gave her time by keeping me in jail.

I didn't want to eat in there. They gave me bologna sandwiches, which I refused, and then they gave me a cup of Kool-Aid, which I also refused. When they saw that I was not eating, they sent me to a mental doctor. The doctor asked me if I wanted to kill myself, and I said no, and he asked me why I was not eating. I told him that I wasn't sure. I did not know what could have been in the cup of Kool- Aid, and I didn't know what the meat was in the bread. I told him that I wanted plain bread and water or milk.

An officer put me in a bigger cell with more women and said, "Here is your water and plain bread. What do you think this is, Burger King? That you can have it your way?"

The first cell I was in had about ten women, most of them Chinese. I knew they were locked up for selling bootleg tapes, so it wasn't so bad—no hardened criminals to deal with. They were more afraid of me. The officers gave us two plastic bags, and I told them to put our garbage in the bag and not on the floor. Then I took one of the bags, told them not to come near me, and made a bed with the plastic bag and my coat. One girl tried to lie on it with me, but I wrapped it around me and went to sleep in a corner for the two nights. Then everybody got out of that cell. I was the only one left, so they took me out and put me in a bigger cell with more women. I took my plastic bed with me. This cell contained a bad bunch of mostly stupid young women.

Officer Green came back and asked me why was I still there, and I told her I didn't know. I became angry because everyone that came in after me was gone. At least now I had someone in there who cared about me. God bless Officer Green for looking into why they had me there so long. She came back to me and said, "Your records were missing so no one could find you." I asked her what that meant, and she said that I got someone mad at me and that person "lost" my records. She said, "Let's go, Cynthia. We're going home." I thanked her profusely. I knew they tried to keep me in the mental ward, but thank God I was seeing the judge.

When I got to see the judge and my husband and loving cousins, I wanted to cry. The judge asked my lawyer why I was beating on a seven-year-old girl, and my stunned lawyer replied that she was not seven but twenty-seven. The judge went on to explain that all the paperwork that he had read indicated that the person I beat up was a seven-year-old girl. The judge asked me if I knew the person, and I replied yes and said that she was my daughter. He asked me why I beat her, and I told him it was because she was a drunk and refused to get help; she wouldn't take care of her children either. He told me that I couldn't be going around beating up on people, and he ordered me to go to anger management. He told me that I was not allowed to go to my house. When I told the judge that I paid the mortgage and the bills and owned the house, he told me that I was not allowed to return there or I would be locked up again. He asked me for an address for where I would be going, and I gave him my brother John's address on 162nd Street. He told me that the case would be going to trial. I was not worried because I figured Nicky would forget about me and get out of my life.

Lamar got me a lawyer, our cousin Desmond. Thank God for Desmond. I had never met him before, but it was a good thing we had Desmond in the family. This was the best thing to happen to me at this time. I hired Desmond, and it wasn't long before we went to court three times and it was over. The case was dropped because Bunnie never came. She told Kemp that she just wanted to see me pay out of my ass for hitting her. I knew that she was going to get it back because I gave her everything and she still wanted me to take care of her adult ass. No freaking way! She needed to grow up.

I had a bad experience with going to jail, but it showed me that I could never have anything to do with this girl named Bunnie, for she was very much against her mother, who didn't do anything wrong to her in life. She was just a mean witch who didn't like me because I didn't want her to be a bum on the streets, but now she had her own children. She would one day understand why I always told her the street life was not good. I never knew she loved the streets so much and had a ghetto madness about herself. I hoped for her children's sake that one day she got some sense and acquired some class.

# Dirty Friends

I was out of jail and the case was thrown out, but I couldn't get into any more trouble because I went to jail one time for beating up Deanna in 1998. That was because she was a stupid bitch who knew Kemp was cheating on me with Sandra. She took that opportunity to be friends with Sandra. Deanna had two faces, whereas I had thought she was my friend. She was the second bitch to cut my throat. She stayed friends with that bitch Sandra because Kemp was fixing her car. That bitch lost a good friend when she crossed me. She began to make prank calls to my house, and I traced the calls. The voice sounded just like Deanna's, and she kept saying, "Bitch, I got your man. Come get him. When I traced the calls, I saw that they came from her work. I called her boss and said that I was going to have her locked up on the job because she was prank calling my house. He fired her ass that day!

Then one day JR ran away because he wanted an Averex jacket that cost eight hundred dollars and I told him no. He ran straight to Deanna's house and hid there. Not much later, she went past my house and I asked her where JR was. She was already mad at me because when I locked Kemp up, she had her car in my garage and I told her that she was going to have to take her car back down the block to her garage so Kemp could fix it there. She yelled at me that day. It was all about her car—she didn't care that he'd pulled those guns on me—and that's when I told her she was not a friend because all she cared about was how she was going to get the car fixed. Then she went and helped JR hide from me. When I asked her where he was, she said, "Fuck you." She told me I was a crazy bitch because I got rid of a good man. She said that now my kids hated me, and I punched her in the mouth. She grabbed me by my hair, and I grabbed her by hers. She had a nice hairdo, and I pulled most of the braids from her head. Let's just say I whipped that ass. She began walking backward, saying to me, "You got that; you got that." But I did not feel as if I got that, so I kicked her in the stomach and knocked her ass to the ground.

I don't know why I beat her so bad, but I think it was everything that she had said to me over the years. She treated me like shit. She always talked down to me, was always condescending.

I had to watch what I was doing because she tried to sue me for fucking up her face. She kept telling people that she was going to sue me and take my house. She was living in the projects with me when I lived there, but she had more education than I did. Her boyfriend, Wiz, never married her, and he bought a house and never put her name on it. She stayed on welfare, and Wiz worked because he didn't trust her lazy welfare all. She loved to party too much, and he knew that. She also liked getting high all the time, so I had to stop hanging out with her and Tina. They were bitches. They only wanted to hang out and get high. I had to pay the court one thousand dollars toward the battered women's foundation just because I whipped that ass. She asked for it. She could have sued me for my house, so I was lucky, but I had two assault cases now, in the cases of Deanna and Nicky. I had to watch my ass and stay out of trouble, but you know by now that trouble always finds me.

Things became quiet and started going well. I sold many homes, and I was still driving the bus. I was making good money now, and I bought Kemp a Mercedes. He and I found a house on Garden City Street. Kemp hated the house and did not want it. Valerie from my office at Cozy Homes Realty helped me find it. She was my real estate agent because I could not sell myself a house. It needed a lot of work, but I loved it.

# Need Kemp Like a Hole in the Head

I have a friend named Joy who drives busses with me. She's so nice and is crazy like me. I became close to her when her son died. I felt bad for her because her son was only twenty-three years old, and because of Georgia, I knew how it was to lose a child. We also had the love of riding motorcycles in common. She helped me find Kemp a job with a bus company. It was a good job, but something was not right with him. He'd come home after drinking on the job, and I thought he was a show-off with his car. It was nearly time to close on the house, and Kemp had been on the job for a couple of months. I was now selling houses like crazy. Most of the bus drivers at the job wanted me to sell them a house. I have to say that I had a good reputation at the job. Everything looked good for now.

I moved into my beautiful big old house. I had yard space for all my crazy brothers and sisters. I'd missed them so much. I hadn't had a BBQ in a couple of years because I spent money on my vacation, the new car for Kemp, new furniture, and now this new house, God bless it. I moved into the new house and started doing work to it. The first thing I had to do was put up a new fence, which cost thousands of dollars. I think it was well worth it. It made the house look so much better, and the neighbors came over to tell me so. I didn't say much to any of them except the ones next door. The house sat on a 120-by-100-foot lot on a nice corner, so there was lots of yard space. I sold three houses out here with me to bus drivers, and they loved it too.

I had to travel an hour with good traffic and an hour and a half with bad traffic to get to work. I had to leave the house at one thirty to be at work by three. I would get back home around midnight because my hours were from three to eleven at night. I loved those hours.

Kemp only had a twenty-minute commute. When we were in Queens, Kemp came home early, but now something had him coming home late.

I had a little money saved and was going to IKEA to buy something for the house. I asked Kemp to take me one Saturday. He took me, but he sat outside in the car while I went into the store. When I came out of the store, I saw him laughing hard with somebody on the phone, and he kept looking around to see if I was coming out of the store. He didn't see that I was standing right next to the car watching him. I asked him who was he talking to, and he said his friend JR. I took the phone from him and redialed the number. A woman answered. I asked her who she was, and she said that she was Kemp's friend Debra. I asked Kemp who Debra was, and he said that he did not know who I was talking to. While Debra was on the phone, I asked him why was he doing this to me, and he swore that he was not doing anything. I asked her how she knew Kemp, and she said that he fixed her car. I hung up and smacked him in the face, and he held my hands. I began to kick the shit out of him. Kemp was telling me that she was just someone that he worked with and that he fixed her car. I redialed Debra and asked if she was just speaking with my husband, and she said yes. Kemp was screaming that she was a liar, insisting that he was talking to JR. He said that he was talking to Debra earlier in the day. I told her to meet me at his job, and she said she would, but she didn't. She probably knew that I wanted to meet me in order to kick her ass. I knew that she and Kemp were on the phone laughing to each other like lovers, not friends.

The asshole Kemp took me home and told me he was friends with her but did not want to tell me because he knew I would get crazy. He was a damn liar, and I knew it. When I got home, I called Joy and told her that Kemp was screwing a girl at the job she got him. She did not believe that Kemp was so sneaky, and I never asked him again about her because he never left the house, but he was telling me he had to work overtime.

I knew he was a liar, but I got sick again and had other things to worry about. He began staying out later and later. He knew I was sick and didn't give a damn. I really needed him at this time, yet he failed. If he got sick, I was going to leave his ass just as he left me. I'd known about Kemp with Debra when we lived in Queens. I just could not find out what he was doing and who he was doing it with. I'd told Tori and Joy when we were living there that Kemp was not having sex with me. I knew he was seeing someone, but I had to make money to get out of Queens. While I was busting my ass driving that bus at night and selling houses in the day, Kemp was working during the day and screwing Debra in the evening.

When we moved to Long Island in August 2006, I hit a pothole. I could not get out of the bed, so I went to the doctor and had an MRI in December of that year. The MRI showed that I had three herniated discs, and I just took painkillers and went back to work. I worked until February 2007. Although I went home, I never got better. I stayed in bed from February 2007 until I had to get emergency surgery on November 27 of that year. I then had an operation on my spine. I had one disc replaced with titanium and had a cage holding my spine up. Without the cage, my spine would have dropped like a cabbage layer. I had four rods, four plates, and four screws. I was walking the day after the operation, but I spent four days in the hospital. It was a great recovery. I loved my doctor, Rafiy. He was an angel sent from heaven. I knew God loved me because although I had titanium rods and screws in my back, I was blessed to be walking. My life had changed so much, and now I couldn't drive a bus anymore. I hadn't sold real estate since I my injury. I lost my savings, and I almost lost the house. However, Sunny and my new daughter-in-law, Nicky, were taking care of me.

When I came home from the hospital, I asked God to help me. He sent me Sunny and Nicky. I'd talked to Sunny before my operation and told him that his father was running the streets and getting drunk with other women. I knew this poor boy was tired of us, hearing that same bullshit he'd heard most of his life. I really hated to tell him, but I knew that he would see it once he came home from the Job Corps. I needed Sunny to know why, and it wasn't because I was sick and had no job and no money.

It was because I really wanted to get away from Kemp because I was sick of him. I wanted to have peace of mind. I was tired of running behind him. It became so bad that I was in the bed and home all day and night. I felt I was losing my mind. I thought Kemp had no heart. Before the operation, I had to cook while I was in pain. Kemp never helped me clean the house or cook. He stayed out all night after work.

I didn't know for sure what was going on, but he left his job at the bus company, which made me think that maybe he wasn't cheating on me. Boy, was I wrong. Now he was driving for another bus company and not making enough to take care of us. He was coming home drunk more. I began watching for his phone bills, but he stopped them from coming to the house. I told him that after my surgery, things were going to change. I think that he thought that I was bullshitting him. He'd had phone calls coming in on his phone a few months prior to my surgery, and I knew it was that bitch Debra. This made it two years, from 2005 to 2007, and she was still calling Kemp. I called her back on his phone and told her that when I caught up with her, she was going to get her ass beat. I had a lot of hate for this woman because she was bold enough to tell me that she was his friend and that she could do anything she wanted with him because I couldn't walk. Her saying that took me to the highest point of anger I had ever experienced.

She knew that I couldn't walk that I had an operation because while I was in recovery after the surgery, Kemp left me in the hospital after visiting me for only half an hour. He was on the phone with her for an hour. I later found that out because it was on his phone bill. He was calling her ten to fifteen times a day. Some days he never called me, and his phone bill proved it.

When Sunny came from the Job Corps, he had to take a test for Con Edison. Kemp took him to the test site, and we did not hear from him all day, from seven in the morning until five that afternoon. After five, he called us and said his phone was not working, but he was a liar like always. When he came home, I beat the shit out of him. Poor Sunny and Nicky came home to fighting between Kemp and me, which occurred every time they saw us together.

Duke, Kemp's son from a previous relationship, came to live with us. Before Sunny even came home, Duke knew his father was cheating on me. He heard me argue with his father for being out on the streets, and he knew his father had other women calling him. At first, Duke didn't believe me, but Duke, Sunny, and Nicky began to see the real Kemp. The night after my surgery, Kemp came from the hospital and was outside on the phone with Debra for an hour. Sunny said he wanted to know why his father was on the phone so long outside.

When I went to the hospital, Kemp did not take me, and when I came home, Kemp never took me for follow-up appointments. He didn't even know the name of the doctor who did my surgery or what they had to do to me. He only found out by looking at the X-rays that I had.

I went to get my stitches taken out, and I came home and saw that he remembered that our twenty-fifth wedding anniversary of being married was approaching. The day was December 13, and all hell began breaking loose at six thirty, when his bitch called him and yelled, "Why did you leave, motherfucker!" I asked him who was yelling at him on the phone and calling him that. He said that it was someone on his job because he left a bus unfinished. I knew he was a liar, so I redialed the phone, but it would not go through. I threw a peanut jar at him, but it missed him. He stayed downstairs. I calmed down because I couldn't go downstairs easily. I heard him come up the stairs a bit later and grabbed another jar of peanut butter to throw at him. It did not hit him, but he grabbed me and punched me in the head. The officer told Sunny to call Kemp and tell him to turn himself in. When Sunny called him, he told our son that he did not hit me, but we all knew that he was a liar. The officers told me to get dressed and come with them to the precinct to press charges against Kemp. This time I did.

He walked in at one in the morning, and I told him I hated him. I asked the police officer to get my house keys for me from the fucker's pockets. He'd left his Jeep in front of the police station, and if I were a bitch, I could have taken that too, but I left it alone. I really wanted to see what was going to happen with him and his bitch. I surely saw that she wanted nothing to do with him other than use him for sex.

She had his head full of shit. I later found out from him that she picked him up from jail and brought him to the police station to get his car. He told me that after he started shit with me about her. You would think he would have enough sense to stay away from her, but no, that's not how Kemp worked. He was going to do anything to get back to his Jeep, and he didn't care if he had to use her to do it. He was a motherfucker. She didn't know Kemp was a user. She picked him up and dropped his ass off and let him live in someone's basement. She told me one time on the phone that she did not date black men, but she was a liar because he was not giving her anything else. He was still bringing me his checks, so the only thing he was giving her was sex. I heard that she was trailer park trash. I believed it because I didn't think that a woman with three children could be so stupid and get nothing but sex from him. Even if she was pretty, she was an ass because she did not care about herself.

I told the jackass Kemp never to come back to my house. He tried, but I let his ass feel that fucking basement apartment that he was living in. He asked me for some blankets, and I sent JR and Sunny with clothes and blankets. He told JR that he was sorry because the woman was living in her house with her husband and he was living in a basement without his family. But I knew that the bitch was not married. I found out later that she was telling him that she was married to keep him out of her house. I knew that she was giving him hell. She wanted him to make me think that they were just friends. However, I knew what kind of shit she was putting in his head. He was out of my house now because of her, and I was waiting to see what she was going to do with him. I told him that I wanted to see the phone bills, and he asked me why. I told him that when he gave me the phone bills and I didn't see any phone calls from her, I would let him come back home. He ordered the phone bills, but I had yet to see one. Now I was stuck because I could lose the house, so I told him that if he came back home, I wanted him to go to counseling for domestic violence and alcohol. He called his lawyer and told him that I was letting him back home, but I told Kemp that if I saw something on the phone bill that was going to make me mad, he'd better tell me. I hadn't let him come home yet.

One day I received a phone call from Martin. I told him that Kemp and I had a fight and that I wasn't letting him back in my house. Martin had owed Kemp some money for fixing his car, and he wanted to pay Kemp, so I told Martin that he could talk to him. I told him to call his cell phone.

Martin called me back the next day and said that his niece wanted to talk to me. She said, "Hi, Cynthia. I wanted to tell you something that happened to me with Kemp." She said that when Kemp was fixing her car, he told her that he wanted to be with her. She said she told him that she knew his wife. He told her that he did not care, but she still told him no. She said that sometime later in the week, she saw Kemp at the train station waiting for her, and because she still owed him money for fixing her car, she asked him if he was there for that. He said no, that he did not want the money, that he wanted her. She told him to go home, but he stayed there and watched her get into her car. She asked him if he was drunk. She said that she was afraid of him because he looked crazy. Apparently, he kept texting her. One text read, "Hi, cutie. Hit me up some time." Another text read, "What's up, cutie? Why won't you call me?" He was like a teenager. Kemp didn't just want Debra.

Debra started to prank call my house. That was my mistake because now I got the phone bills. Kemp came home, and I knew this would not last. I put him out December 13, 2007. I didn't let him come back home until December 31, 2007. I got the mail with the phone bill the same day he came back. I could not believe my eyes when I saw the calls he was making to that bitch Debra.

He called her 110 times within the time that I kicked him out. I faxed it to his entire family, but they already knew how he was. I called him at work, saying that he should have told me about this because I did not want to be surprised like this. I told him not to come back to my fucking house. I hated him for the bills most because it was showing me that the bitch was getting with him all the time as if she were the wife. I made his breakfast at six in the morning and packed his lunch for him; he was out the door at six thirty; and he was on the phone with her every morning. He was also on the phone with her from the moment he left work until he pulled up to the house. Now he was turning his phone off until midnight, when he would call her. I figured he was calling her in the bathroom. I could never catch him on the phone with her; he was very sneaky. I didn't understand how he thought she was married when he was on the phone with her all day. She drove a school bus and worked from six in the morning until nine in the morning; from nine to one, she was doing nothing but talking to a jackass. He was on the phone at work. I didn't know how he worked. He seldom called me, and the only times he did, he wanted to know what I was cooking and if the grass was being watered.

Now that I had the phone bills, I didn't want him home; there was nothing there for him. However, I had to take him back in because I had no money, no job. Now it was time for him to take care of me. He was still going to counseling, and I was doing a little better.

I was called in to be a station agent, and I began training. They had us doing scars, which is when the railroad agent does not handle money but stays outside of the booth. On our first day out after the four-week training, they instructed me to go to Roosevelt Island to give the people information about the tram being out for repairs.

# Back on My Feet

The doctor from transit knew I couldn't stand on my feet for hours. How could anyone expect me to? It was now June 2008, just six months after my surgery. Therefore, when I got to Roosevelt Island, I sat down. When the supervisor asked me why I was sitting down, I told her that I had spinal surgery and that I could not stand for eight hours. She said okay and took me to medical. They sent me right back home, where I waited for the doctors to tell me when I could return to work. I had to work seven more years before I could think about retirement, which would be the time my life changed for the better and I wouldn't be making it with Kemp.

I had enough talk about Kemp. I was very sad about my relationship going bad. I had JR for my first husband, and he was my first boyfriend and the father of three of my children. I had Marley, a bad mistake but nothing to regret. Then I met Kemp, the worst thing in my life, which was the third strike. But I got one nice son from him, Sunny. Even though he was Kemp's son, he was a blessing. Then I got mixed up with Egypt—bad move. This madman wanted to make Kemp understand that there was someone out there to love me other than him. There was a time when I would say "tit for tat" to Egypt, and he always asked me what this meant. I always responded that he didn't need to know. But when we split, he knew what it meant. He said it to me when we split. He knew that I was trying to pay Kemp back for doing so many things to me.

Back in 1998, I went to my medical doctor because I was going through a bad depression and had vertigo. My doctor asked me what was making me so sick, and I told him it was Kemp. He said to weigh the good and the bad and if there was more good, then I should stay and deal with it, and he said if there was more bad, then I should get out soon. I never listened because it was more bad than good with Kemp. The list was short as far as his being good.

| Good | Bad |
|---|---|
| Sex | Cheats on me every year |
| Nice gifts sometimes | Doesn't remember my birthday |
| Brings home paycheck | Doesn't remember our anniversary |
| Great mechanic | Cannot trust him |
| | Liar, all of the time |
| | Doesn't call his mother |
| | Doesn't call me unless he needs me |
| | Doesn't do home repairs |
| | Drinks |
| | Follows bad people |
| | Doesn't act like a father |
| | Likes to have every dream car |
| | Thinks he's perpetually twenty |
| | Acts as if he does not care |
| | Likes nasty movies |
| | Doesn't spend time with his mother |
| | Doesn't remember his mother's birthday |
| | Respects women that he cheats with and not his wife |
| | Doesn't takes me anywhere |

I could go on forever about that man. Every time Sunny did something that made me angry, I'd get on him because I didn't want him to be like his father. Sunny was a liar like Kemp, but about small stupid things. However, I didn't want him to grow up being a liar about anything big or small. One thing I could say was that Sunny was a fair and kind person. He was very sweet, which he got from me. He would be the best husband because he had a kind heart and was understanding.

# Lies and Trust

My relationships were never perfect, but I thanked God that I wasn't in this wasn't in this big world by myself.

Sunny was blessed with his wife, Nicky. When I was lying in my hospital bed, I kept thanking God for the great woman Sunny married. I thought he got a woman just like his mother, so I tell you, he'd better treat her like a queen. She came to me as if she were my daughter. I was praying for them to give me grandchildren.

Nicky had gotten better. I thanked God that I had her and would do anything for her. She took care of me when I came home after my surgery. I was always sitting on my bed crying about what good she did for me. I loved her very much, and that was from my heart. If I had money, I would take her and Sunny all over the world just to show her and him how much I thanked God for them. I'd never do anything to hurt them, and I knew Sunny, Nicky, and JR were all I had in my life, in addition to my brothers and sisters.

When I was in the operation room, I didn't want to cry, but when I looked back at Sunny and my brother John, I knew I had to come out of this well just for them. I loved my brother John so much that words could not express what love I had for him. He was the biggest gift and friend. I knew he was sent from God. This was the reason I went on in life. My life stayed strong when I looked at my brother and my sons. I knew what my brother went through, and I never wanted to know that he hurt like that again. When I came home from the hospital, I wanted to take my brother and sons far from Kemp and live somewhere in peace. I would be able to one day.

There was more to my life than Kemp, and I had to go through a lot with him to know this. He was now sick with colon problems.

He was making out okay because I was still taking good care of him.

Again, Nicky had become a sweet and respectful daughter, and this made me happy. She now had a new baby and was taking great care of herself and her children. She was a real mother to her children now. She stopped running the streets and was into enjoying her mother and children. We had family get-togethers and time out with each other as mother and daughter. I wanted to take my daughter on a trip out of the country so she could see the world and know other people, places, and things. We had the mother and daughter relationship that I always saw my friends have and never did. I loved it.

My mother was my friend too, but she got sick with those pills and forgot I was there half the time.

I had a good relationship with my stepmother. She truly showed me everything I knew as an adult woman. Now she was getting old and forgetting a lot. She was still caring about me, and I loved her for this. I took her out as much as I could, but she couldn't awl so well now.

My father and I had a great relationship too. On my days off, my stepmother, father, and brother Mike spent time with me.

I had so many brothers and sisters that I didn't have time for all of them. My oldest brother, Bob, and my brothers Tim and Dan were all from my father and had different mothers. Bob was one of my darling brothers. Tim died before I could spend any time with him. Dan stayed away from everyone. I'd only seen him one time in my life, and that was at my nephew's funeral—Tim's baby son.

We never see Tom because he lived in Georgia. We were always at the house with my father and mother but didn't see each other much as adults. John was the brother who was very close to me. We did everything together. I never saw my sister Pam. I'd like to spend more time with her, but she lived in the Bronx. Duke, one of the funniest brothers we had, was a clown. He was in Florida. Jack and I talked every day. He was also in Florida. His twin, Jake, was a strange and religious person. He was close to me when he was a young boy, but he changed. He was good friends with Kemp and did not have much to say to me when he stopped by the house. He lived about thirty minutes from me. Susan lived in California, and I would love to see her because I hadn't seen her since she left New York years ago. Kate lived in the Bronx, and I never saw her, but I would love to spend more time with her. Patty lived in Brooklyn, and I only saw her on Thanksgiving. She saw my daughter, Nicky, more often. My daddy didn't see her either because my stepmom wanted her out of his life because she never believed that she was his child, but that's another story. My stepmother thought that only Mike, Tom, and I were are my father's children, but that's another story too. My uncle is said to be John, Pam, and Duke's father. Yes, my father's own brother. I wish they would take a blood test because many people were mad at my mother and father. I never talked about this to anyone, but this was bad blood between us. My father told me the story of how he thought that my mother cheated on him with his brother and had John, Pam, and Duke. That was so sad to me. I told my brothers and sisters, and they did not care what my father said. I asked them to take a blood test, but the ugly eye-rolling and not talking about it continued. It would always go on until they knew the truth.

My stepmother passed away at eighty-two years of age, and my mother had been dead since 1990. My father was eighty-seven years old but still going strong. I guessed we would never find out if any of his children weren't actually his, and these brothers and sisters of mine were not as curious as I was to know. I remembered so much sometimes. I wanted to forget, but things stayed in my head.

I used to hate looking at mayonnaise jars because doing so reminded me of when my mother lost a baby in the toilet when I was about eight or nine. She wanted to take the baby out of the toilet, so she told me to go into the kitchen to get her any kind of empty jar. I looked all over the kitchen for an empty jar and then took an empty mayonnaise jar to the bathroom, where I watched her take the tiny fetus out of the toilet. It looked like a baby chicken with no feathers. She told me to watch my brothers and sisters because she had to go to the hospital because the baby was dead. I was so shocked, but I didn't cry. Maybe because I didn't understand what had really happened. All day long, John, Tom, and Pam asked me where Mommy was, but she told me not to tell them because she didn't want my father to know.

After that, baby Duke was born, and I loved him so much. I remembered that Mommy was very sick when she had Duke. I had to stay home so much with her to take care of him that I was left back in the fourth grade. My teacher told Mommy that if this kept happening, her children were going to be taken away from her. I remember her telling me that she would never let that happen again. At one point, we'd moved into the American Legion, and she stayed with this white man named Clarke. He was her new boyfriend. My brothers and sisters used to be teased about Clarke because the kids knew my father and would ask who Clarke was. We told them the truth, that he was my mother's boyfriend because my father left my mother.

We moved so much, and I came to Coney Island with my mother, but when she died, I hated it because so many bad things happened there; however, the kids loved it because of the rides. I always told myself that when I got the chance to leave Coney Island, I would never look back. I remember how my grandmother cut my step-grandfather's nose with the same knife that she used to cut up cabbage. I hated East New York because of that baby sis or bro that mommy lost in the toilet. I think that's why I had bad relationships and my children didn't care about me.

Now that I'm getting older and the things I used to go through have stopped, my life is very calm. I don't understand why I went through this; I was not a drunk or a junkie. I guess I was blessed more than I knew. Thank God for my health. My brothers and sisters are all healthy, and my children and grandchildren are healthy too. I have wonderful grandchildren!

| My Brothers | My Sisters |
|---|---|
| Bob—Father | Pam—Father and Mother |
| Tim—Father | Susan—Mother |
| Dan—Father | Kate—Mother |
| Tom—Mother and Father | Patty—Father and Mother |
| John—Mother and Father | |
| Duke—Mother and Father | |
| Jack—Mother | |
| Jake—Mother | |

What does it mean to have all of these brothers and sisters? I always wanted to know, but that didn't stop me from loving them very much. I wanted to let my kids know that they should love each other as much as I love my brothers and sisters, if not more. Even if we had a dysfunctional family with our parents and grandparents, I think I was blessed to have that special bond between all of us siblings.

I want to let my stepmother know how much I love her, and I think that when she was alive, I did show her that I love her very much. I want my brothers and sisters, my children, and my grandchildren to know that I love them all very much, but I think most of them know.

To all the women I know and do not know, this is for you. I want the women who go through so much pain in their lives to know that someone loves them too. My girlfriends, I love you all. I wrote this book to let you all know that there is more to life than a relationship with man. It begins with God and ends with God because he loves us.

# About the Author

The author was born in Brooklyn. She is one of fifteen children. She is a transit employee as well as a real estate agent. Aileen has always been known to have the gift of gab. She's also been known to be an excellent storyteller, and she has interesting stories to tell.

Printed in the United States
By Bookmasters